A SHOWER OF LEAD

The gunman that had been about to fire spun in a quick, tight semicircle as if one of his legs had been suddenly kicked out from under him. His face was etched with surprise, and he squeezed off his shot more from shock than anything else.

The remaining three gunmen at the table watched in amazement as their partner was twisted around like a rag doll. When they saw the bloody wound in the man's thigh, all three of them looked back at the one who'd done the shooting.

Holding the smoking Colt in his hand, Clint couldn't tell if the man with the shotgun was actually coming to his senses or had simply been thrown toward the floor. The other three were turning their sights on him. All at once, they took aim and started squeezing their triggers.

A storm descended upon that saloon, complete with thunder and a hail of lead . . .

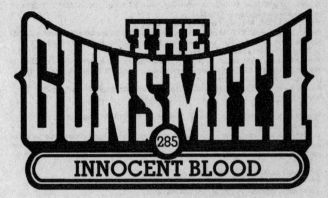

THE GUNSMITH

285

INNOCENT BLOOD

J. R. ROBERTS

J

JOVE BOOKS, NEW YORK

THE BERKLEY PUBLISHING GROUP
Published by the Penguin Group
Penguin Group (USA) Inc.
375 Hudson Street, New York, New York 10014, USA
Penguin Group (Canada), 90 Eglinton Avenue East, Suite 700, Toronto, Ontario M4P 2Y3, Canada
(a division of Pearson Penguin Canada Inc.)
Penguin Books Ltd., 80 Strand, London WC2R 0RL, England
Penguin Group Ireland, 25 St. Stephen's Green, Dublin 2, Ireland (a division of Penguin Books Ltd.)
Penguin Group (Australia), 250 Camberwell Road, Camberwell, Victoria 3124, Australia
(a division of Pearson Australia Group Pty. Ltd.)
Penguin Books India Pvt. Ltd., 11 Community Centre, Panchsheel Park, New Delhi—110 017, India
Penguin Group (NZ), Cnr. Airborne and Rosedale Roads, Albany, Auckland 1310, New Zealand
(a division of Pearson New Zealand Ltd.)
Penguin Books (South Africa) (Pty.) Ltd., 24 Sturdee Avenue, Rosebank, Johannesburg 2196,
South Africa

Penguin Books Ltd., Registered Offices: 80 Strand, London WC2R 0RL, England

INNOCENT BLOOD

A Jove Book / published by arrangement with the author

PRINTING HISTORY
Jove edition / September 2005

ISBN: 0-515-14012-0

JOVE®
Jove Books are published by The Berkley Publishing Group,
a division of Penguin Group (USA) Inc.,
375 Hudson Street, New York, New York 10014.
JOVE is a registered trademark of Penguin Group (USA) Inc.
The "J" design is a trademark belonging to Penguin Group (USA) Inc.

PRINTED IN THE UNITED STATES OF AMERICA

10 9 8 7 6 5 4 3 2 1

ONE

It hadn't rained for over two months, although nobody would have guessed that by looking at the sky or even feeling the ground under his feet. The open country of northern Wyoming stretched out so far that anyone standing in a good spot could see for miles in any direction. The wind had so many places to go that it hardly even bothered the people trying to scratch out their living underneath it.

The winter was on its way, but wasn't quite there yet, and the clouds were so thick that they colored the whole sky a murky gray. Every now and then the sun came out, but only to let folks know what they were missing during the rest of the day. Nighttime frosts were starting up, which kept the dirt and fallen leaves just damp enough to take on an extra chill.

Without taking all of this into account, finding Mary Swann resting with her back against a tree stump might not have seemed too unusual. She was sitting on the ground with her hands folded across her stomach. Her head was leaning back so she could look at the sky with eyes that were just barely open. Her skin glistened a bit and her hair drifted around her young, pretty face as the breeze passed her by.

1

Mary's dress was rumpled, but not any more than you might expect from someone who'd gotten the idea in her head to sit out and try to enjoy a cold, dreary day. Although her stump was a mile or so out of town, plenty of folks saw her in her spot as they ambled down the road heading north toward the Powder River.

Those folks waved to Mary and watched until they saw her nod back. Some of them shouted to her to see if she was cold or needed a ride somewhere, but they got little or no answer in response. Mary liked wandering on her own, so nobody thought much of it.

Nobody, that is, until Jeremiah Swann caught sight of her.

"Mary? Is that you?" Jeremiah called. He saw her head move a bit toward him, but didn't get a reply. Although he'd seen plenty of girls younger than Mary off playing on their own, those girls weren't Jeremiah's concern. They weren't his daughters. Mary was.

"I've been looking all over for you, girl," Jeremiah said as he stepped off the road and walked toward the stump where Mary was resting. "You haven't run off on me like this since you were in pigtails. I swear, a girl your age should know better than to sit on the damp grass like that. You'll catch a fever."

The closer Jeremiah got to his daughter, the wider he smiled. His breath was coming in deeper gusts, but not from the uphill climb he was taking to get to his daughter. It had been a long day already, even though it was barely half over. His hands were callused and blacker than usual after putting in a good amount of time in his shop.

He'd left his hammer and anvil back in town, however, when he didn't get his daily visit from his girl. Mary didn't have to bring him lunch, but she'd done it for so long that Jeremiah had started telling the time of day by when his daughter would come through the door of his shop.

When she was late this day, he'd noticed and had shaken his head. When an hour had passed, he started to wonder if she'd gotten lost. He might have even gotten worried if old Ernie Niedelander hadn't said that he'd seen her on his way into town.

Mary had liked to scout out for miles when she was a kid. Maybe she'd gotten distracted.

"I missed my lunch today," Jeremiah said as he got up close enough to her that he could talk without shouting. "When I heard you were out here, I remember what you said before about wanting to drag me out of my shop someday for a picnic. Today's kind of cold, but I guess there's no better time than the present, right?"

Mary didn't answer.

The wind was playing with the edges of her skirt and tussling her hair. In fact, it seemed that she was stretched out even more than Jeremiah had guessed on his way from the road. She could have even been asleep.

"You getting cold, there?" Jeremiah asked as he knelt down to his daughter's side. Reaching out, he put his hand on top of hers. "You feel cold as ice! You need to get inside before you . . ."

Jeremiah trailed off as the air completely drained from his lungs.

Not only was Mary's skin cold, but it was colder than the wind or even the damp ground under her. It was colder than anything had a right to be.

"Come on now," Jeremiah said, not wanting to play the part of doting father to a girl who was now a young woman. "The last thing we need is for you to get sick. You know how much you hate that tonic you had to drink the last time."

When he nudged her, Jeremiah saw Mary shift a bit against her log. She slid a little ways down and to one side before coming to a jerky stop. Her clothes were bunched up in odd places, mainly since they'd snagged against the bark and were the only things holding her up.

Jeremiah's heart skipped a beat and thoughts rushed

through his mind in a flood. As he reached down to Mary, he sifted through everything that had happened throughout the day. He wondered about the last time he'd seen her and if she'd been all right.

He wondered if she'd seemed happy or frightened.

He then thought back to the last thing he'd said to her when she'd actually answered.

The movements he'd seen before weren't coming from her. That much was plain now. Her hair was brushed in the wind, but there was something else about it, too. It moved enough at times to make it seem as though her head itself was shifting slightly. That was only because her hair was not exactly connected to her head any longer.

"Jesus," Jeremiah muttered as he pushed some of Mary's hair from her face only to find that her skin had been cut just below the hairline.

It wasn't much to see. Just a thin red line that traced over her ears and down across the top of her neck. With just a little testing from his hand, Jeremiah saw that the cut did indeed wrap around the top portion of her head.

His little girl had been scalped.

TWO

Claymore was a small town nestled in a sprawling area of Wyoming. It was the kind of town a man could spot half a day before his horse got him there. Crooked wooden buildings leaned together in neat rows on an otherwise unimpressive landscape. From a distance, the roads leading in and out of town looked more like brown lines scratched into the earth.

There were only two main streets in Claymore, which were only crowded at two times a day. Every now and then a cattle drive would tear through town, but there wasn't one of those due for some time. All in all, it was a peaceful day where the only noise consisted of the occasional wagon wheels rumbling by and the clang of hammer against anvil from the blacksmith's shop.

The hammer had been silent for a while. The blacksmith, on the other hand, was anything but.

"I want justice!" Jeremiah screamed. "Goddammit, someone needs to pay for what happened to my little girl!"

While there was a crowd growing around the burly figure of Jeremiah Swann, the blacksmith didn't seem to notice any of them. Jeremiah had been calm and gentle around his Mary, but after seeing what had been done to her, that picture had drastically changed.

Jeremiah reared up to his full height. Every one of his breaths made his chest swell like the bellows in his own shop. Muscles earned from a lifetime of shaping iron tensed and twitched beneath his scarred flesh. Thick, callused hands curled into fists and tightened until his knuckles were white from the pressure.

When Jeremiah spoke, his mouth gaped open like a hungry animal's behind his thick beard. "Did you see my girl? Did you see what they done to my Mary?"

The one man Jeremiah did seem to notice wasn't a part of the crowd. He was a man of more than average height with a lean, muscular build. Light brown hair was closely cropped, which was a bit of a contrast to the long whiskers sprouting from his upper lip. This man was dressed in a plain, yet well-cared-for suit with a tin star pinned to his lapel.

"I saw what happened to your girl, Jeremiah," the lawman said.

"I don't think you did. If'n you really saw her, you wouldn't be so content to just stand there while the one who done this is still out there drawing breath."

"This is a terrible thing," the lawman said in an attempt to calm Jeremiah down. "There won't be anyone to argue that. But we can't just go off half-cocked until we know who to go after."

The more both men talked, the more the crowd around them started to respond. At first, the others had come to watch the argument the way they might want to see any barroom brawl. Now that they heard what was being said, however, their interest became even more piqued.

"What happened?" asked one person in the crowd.

Another responded with, "Mary Swann's been killed."

"I heard she was gutted."

"No, no. She was skinned," another voice whispered.

Hearing these words get tossed about brought a scowl onto the lawman's face. His brow furrowed and he glared around at the others as if looking for someone to smack across the face.

"There'll be none of that talk," the lawman snarled. "There's been a killing and that's all anyone needs to know right now. For God's sake, her father's right here."

"Yer damn right I'm here," Jeremiah said. "I came to you to see what's to be done about this. I'm a law-abiding man, but I sure as hell ain't going to sit around and wait when I could just pick up and track down that murdering bastard myself."

"We don't take to vigilantes around here, Jeremiah," the lawman warned. "You know that."

"That's fine, but we also don't take to animals that spill innocent blood."

One of the men in the crowd pumped his fist into the air and shouted, "That's right!"

The lawman looked around and didn't like what he saw. The faces that had been curious before were now growing angry and indignant. That simply would not do, especially since the crowd was still growing larger. Hopping onto the boardwalk behind him put the lawman about a head higher than everyone else.

"Look here, now," he said. "This is law business. It don't concern the rest of you. Just go back to what you were doing. Move along, now," he added when he saw that his previous words didn't seem to sink in. "Get going before I get you going myself. I've got plenty to do here, and I'm sure Jeremiah doesn't want me wasting my time trying to get a mob under control."

Although he was still plenty riled up, Jeremiah lowered his head for a moment. If nothing else, it seemed that the lawman's words were affecting somebody.

Seeing the look in the lawman's eyes as well as how close his hand was to his pistol, the crowd grumbled a bit more to themselves before splitting off in their various directions. Once he saw that the group had been sufficiently broken up, the lawman hopped back down from the boardwalk so he could stand in front of Jeremiah.

"I heard what you said," Jeremiah told him. "And I respect it. But my girl is dead." Those last words stuck in his throat, but Jeremiah pushed through them all the same. "If you don't plan on doing something about it, Sheriff, then I will."

The sheriff reached out to put both his hands on Jeremiah's shoulders. "Of course I'm going to do something about it, Jeremiah. I only just heard about this a few minutes ago. You need to pull yourself together and let me do my job. Maybe you should head over to Kylie's and get something to drink."

"And maybe you should head down there with me. There's plenty of scum there that'd kill their own mommas for a dime. My guess is one of them strangers did this to my girl."

"All right, then. I'll see you over there and I'll get started on looking into this. Agreed?"

"For now," Jeremiah replied, shaking the hand the sheriff offered. "But I won't sit still for too long."

"I wouldn't expect you to. In fact, I may need you and all the able gunhands I can muster once I flush out this murdering bastard."

THREE

Jeremiah never took anything in stride. Good or bad, full or flush, he was a fighter. Even when things were at their best, he fought to make sure they stayed that way. Now that his life had dropped to the lowest point it had ever been, he had more fire in him than even he would have thought possible.

Although he followed through on the sheriff's request, the last thing Jeremiah planned on doing was sitting still and waiting for the lawman to find him. Mary was still dead. She would always be dead. And Jeremiah would always be enraged by that.

He'd listened to enough sermons. He'd read the Good Book from cover to cover. He knew that vengeance was a lost cause and that it might even damn his own soul. At that moment, however, he just didn't care about any of that.

Vengeance was all he had.

Kylie's wasn't the only saloon in town, but it was the one that was easiest to find. Because of that, it drew most of the strangers that came to Claymore, as well as a good amount of gamblers and gunfighters. Those were the types who wanted more than a drink and a meal. Those were the ones looking to ply their wicked trades or make a name for themselves.

9

Those were the men that Jeremiah was after.

Storming into the saloon like a twister ravaging a farmstead, Jeremiah shoved through the front door and stomped right over to the bar. Like most of the folks who'd lived in Claymore for most of their lives, Jeremiah knew the barkeep at Kylie's well enough. He also knew more than just the older fellow's name.

"Jeremiah, I heard about Mary," the barkeep said. "Anything you want, it's on the house."

"That's good of you, Sal," Jeremiah said to the barkeep. "But I know exactly what I want."

Before the older man behind the bar could do anything else, he was practically shoved back into the racks of bottles behind him. Even as he caught himself before knocking anything over, Sal looked as though he could scarcely believe what was happening.

"Didn't Sheriff Hayes see you yet?" Sal asked.

Jeremiah was leaning over the bar and reaching down behind it with one hand. "Yeah. I spoke to him."

"Then maybe you should just—" Sal's eyes went wide and his words caught in the back of his throat once he got a look at what Jeremiah was after. "Jesus Christ, what're you doing?"

After a bit of grasping behind the bar, Jeremiah's hand found the sawed-off shotgun that was kept there. Despite the fact that Sal hadn't even winged more than a handful of drunks or rowdies in his life, the damage done to the ceiling, floor and furniture around Sal's post showed that the gun was fired plenty of times. Enough times, at least, for any local to know where it was kept.

"I'm doing what needs to be done," Jeremiah replied grimly. When he saw Sal starting to reach out to reclaim the shotgun, Jeremiah shifted a deadly gaze in his direction. "Don't try to stop me, either."

Sal froze where he was, one hand extended toward the shotgun. Once he got a good look at Jeremiah's face, he retracted his arm and took an additional step back. "Just be sure about what you're doing," Sal warned. "Think about your own future."

As he turned around, Jeremiah checked to make sure the shotgun was loaded and then shut it with a snap of his wrist. "I ain't got no more future."

When he turned around, Jeremiah saw that he'd already managed to grab the attention of everybody in the room. As long as they weren't slumped over in a corner or face-down at a table, they were looking at Jeremiah with bated breath.

Bringing the shotgun up, Jeremiah slowly moved it so he could aim at anyone he looked at. "Which one of you sons of bitches hurt my little girl?" he asked the entire saloon.

Jeremiah looked at each face in turn. Some of them, he recognized. Most of them, he didn't. The familiar faces were quickly passed over. At the moment, Jeremiah was obviously addressing the strangers.

The shotgun in Jeremiah's hand didn't tremble.

His eyes were like pieces of coal that were just shy of hardening into diamonds.

His mouth was a grim line, and the words that came from it were pushed out in a harsh whisper.

"I know plenty of you are killers," Jeremiah said. "Own up to what you done. If you're tough enough to kill a woman and do what you did, then you're tough enough to take the consequences."

When he didn't get anything besides silent stares in return, Jeremiah started to get even madder. That much was obvious by the burning intensity that flared up in his eyes and the twitch at the corner of his mouth.

"All right, then," Jeremiah said. "I'll just go with what I know." He walked through the saloon, keeping the shotgun pointed in front of him. Kicking chairs and nudging tables out of his way, he herded most of the bodies in Kylie's into one half of the room.

"You don't want to do this," one man said from a table at the back.

"Shut yer mouth, mister," Jeremiah snapped. "I'll be getting to you soon enough."

When he got to a specific table, Jeremiah stopped and planted his feet so they were shoulder width apart. His eyes darted toward every noise he heard, even if it was a cough or a glass scraping against a wooden surface. Jeremiah's hands clenched around the shotgun and his finger moved along the trigger as though he was tracing the edge of a blade.

"You," Jeremiah said, focusing on the dirty face of a stranger who'd been playing cards. "I heard you were kicking up trouble from the moment you got here. You say you're a killer and I heard you're none too kind to women that cross your path."

The man stared arrogantly into the barrel of the shotgun. "I don't know what the hell you're blabbing about," he grunted. "I been here all night and I don't know nothing about yer wife or daughter or whoever it is that's got you all riled up."

Jeremiah's eyes narrowed. "Is that so?"

"He's right, Jeremiah," Sal said from behind the bar. "For God's sake, put the gun down and let Sheriff Hayes handle this."

"This man's a killer," Jeremiah said.

"True or not, he's been sitting in that chair for the better part of two days," Sal said. "I can swear to that."

"Fine. What about the rest of these bastards?"

"They all been playing there at the same game for all this time. Ask anyone in here."

Looking around to a few select faces, Jeremiah got some frightened nods in return. He slowly nodded and worked his way past the table. The shotgun was still firmly in his grasp.

"Then I might as well talk to you," Jeremiah said. "Since you seem to be the one that wants to talk to me."

The man who'd spoken up first was still in his seat in the back. When he saw Jeremiah approach, he stood up and held his hands out to the sides. "You're making a mistake. Whatever happened, this won't help."

For a moment, it seemed as if Jeremiah was listening. He then scowled, cleared his throat and spit at the man's feet. "I know you're a killer. You're a famous killer, and if you didn't hurt my girl then you know who did. I heard you killed more men than the pox, so I might as well rid the world of you and be done with it."

Clint Adams kept his hands held high and his face calm as he studied the man holding him at gunpoint. From what he could tell, he had about three seconds to find a good way out of this.

After that, it was going to get messy.

FOUR

Clint's mind raced and his hand itched to take hold of the modified Colt at his side. He didn't know this man in front of him and he didn't want to hurt anyone. But he knew a few other things as well.

First of all, Clint knew that the man holding the shotgun wasn't in his right mind.

Second, Clint knew that only made it more likely that the man would pull the shotgun's trigger and ask questions later.

"I heard of you," Jeremiah repeated in a wavering voice. "You're The Gunsmith."

"Some have called me that," Clint said.

"And you're a killer."

"I've killed men, but that doesn't make me a killer."

"What's the difference?"

"I act when I need to, but I don't set out to hurt anyone. Actually, I'd say we both have that very thing in common."

Jeremiah stood about four paces away from Clint. Holding that shotgun in his hands seemed to close a good portion of that distance, however. The fact that his finger was tightening slowly around the trigger did that even more.

"Maybe I can help you," Clint said.

"Why the hell would I want your help?"

"It looks like you need someone's help. How about you put that gun down and tell me what happened to your daughter?"

Despite the fact that Jeremiah still aimed his shotgun right at Clint's head, something changed that defused a bit of the situation. Something had shifted in Jeremiah's eyes that gave Clint a bit of hope. At the very least, it gave him something to work with.

"Best do as he says, fella," came a voice from the table that had been Jeremiah's first stop. That voice was quickly followed by the sound of a pistol's hammer being snapped back. "We're getting real tired of you flapping your gums and waving that gun in our faces."

Clint could see the men getting up from that table. With Jeremiah directly in front of him, however, he didn't see them draw their guns until it was too late.

Pulling in a breath, Jeremiah swung himself around to point the shotgun back at that other table. "What did you say?"

"You heard him," another of the gunmen replied. "Go back home before we make you eat that shotgun."

Jeremiah shifted his aim between one of the gunmen at the other table and another. The more he moved, the more uncertain his movements became. And the more uncertain he became, the more unsteady he got.

Despite the fact that he'd been in Jeremiah's sights not too long ago, Clint hated to see that shotgun turn toward that other table. If he could see the shakiness in the man's arms, then so could those other gunmen. In fact, to those gunmen, that shakiness was like blood tossed into shark-infested waters.

The gunmen stepped away from their table and fanned out in front of Jeremiah. Another couple of steps later, two of them even started working their way around to flank Jeremiah where he stood.

"I'm warning you," Jeremiah growled. "Stay back or so help me—"

"You'll what?" one of the gunmen challenged. "Shake so hard that you piss yourself?"

While the other three gunmen laughed at that, everyone else in the saloon was looking for a way to get out. People edged toward the door, while some others merely looked around for somewhere to jump for cover.

"We don't like getting threatened by no old men," the first gunman said. "Especially when it's for no good reason."

Another of the gunmen lifted his pistol and said, "So the least we can do is give you a reason."

With that said, all four of the gunmen set themselves where they stood and brought their pistols up to fire. The first one of them to draw was going to be the first one to fire, and he was about to do so, before Jeremiah could point the shotgun in his direction.

A shot blasted through the air and lead whipped past Jeremiah's hip.

That bullet hadn't come from any of the men in front of him, however. Instead, it came from behind him. The sound of the shot echoed through Jeremiah's ears and set them to ringing while everything else exploded around him.

The gunman that had been about to fire spun in a quick, tight semicircle as if one of his legs had been suddenly kicked out from under him. His face was etched with surprise, and he squeezed off his shot more from shock than anything else. One of his legs was burning with pain, and when he tried to set it down again, he toppled over onto his side.

The remaining three gunmen at the table watched in amazement as their partner was twisted around like a rag doll. When they saw the bloody wound in the man's thigh, they knew he'd been shot. Then all three of them looked back at the one who'd done the shooting.

Holding the smoking Colt in his hand, Clint reached out

with his other hand to grab hold of Jeremiah's elbow. First, he pulled the man's arm straight out to one side so his finger was no longer on the shotgun's trigger. Then he kept pulling until Jeremiah was staggering out of Clint's field of vision.

"Get down," Clint ordered.

Clint couldn't tell if the man with the shotgun was actually coming to his senses or had simply been thrown toward the floor. Either way, he was out of the line of fire for the moment. Of course, just because he could see the entire playing field didn't mean that Clint was happy about it.

Since the first gunman had fallen over, the other three were turning their sights toward Clint. All at once, they took aim and started squeezing their triggers.

A storm descended upon that saloon, complete with thunder and a hail of lead.

FIVE

Clint lowered himself to one knee so he could find some cover behind part of a table and a chair. Looking around the side of the chair, he picked out the closest of the gunmen, who seemed to be actually taking the time to aim instead of blindly firing in any direction.

Although his first instinct was to kill the gunmen before they got in a lucky shot, Clint shifted his aim by a fraction of an inch before taking his shot. The modified Colt bucked in his hand, sending a round into the ribs of another gunman.

That gunman let out a grunting curse, grabbed at his bleeding side and tripped backward over a chair.

Two gunmen remained. One of them was trying to scream over the ringing in his ears while the other was stepping forward to where Clint was ducking.

"Come on out of there, you bastard," that gunman snarled.

"Sure," Clint said as he stood up with his gun arm hanging loosely at his side. "Whatever you say."

Whether he knew it or not, this was the other man's chance to make good and leave the saloon in one piece. When he saw that Clint wasn't about to make a move just yet, the gunman looked confused. Then his features took an ugly turn and he brought up his pistol before Clint could say another word.

Clint's hand moved so fast that it didn't seem to move at all. One moment it was straight at his side with the pistol pointed to the floor; the next it was bent so the Colt was spewing smoke and fire at its target.

The gunman in front of Clint jumped back a step, as though someone had pulled him by the back of his belt. He started to take aim again, but found that he no longer had the strength. Looking down, he spotted the bloody hole in his chest.

That was about the time when he realized that he could no longer breathe and that he was falling backward onto the floor. The third gunman was dead before his back hit the floorboards, his heart torn apart by Clint's lead.

"What about you?" Clint asked, turning his eyes toward the fourth gunman while lowering his Colt once again. "You want to walk out of here or do you want to try something stupid like your friends?"

The fourth gunman was the only one in the saloon besides Clint who was still on his feet. One of his partners was grunting under his breath, trying to crawl toward the gun he'd dropped, while dragging his wounded leg behind him. Another partner was still gripping the bloody gash in his side while trying to figure out which way was up. Finally, the fourth gunman's eyes fell upon the body of the final man, whose lifeless eyes gaped up toward the ceiling.

Once he'd taken all of that in, the last gunman standing didn't walk out of Kylie's.

He ran.

Clint holstered the Colt and turned toward Jeremiah. "I think you and I need to have a talk."

SIX

"I don't need to talk to anyone, mister," Jeremiah replied. "Especially not another gunfighter."

"Do I know you?" Clint asked, suddenly showing the frustration that had jumped on him like a bobcat. "Because as near as I can tell, I was just sitting here enjoying a game of poker when you walked in, grabbed a shotgun and started waving it in my face."

Jeremiah looked down at his hands as though he was surprised to find them still wrapped around the shotgun. When he looked up again, the edge that had been there before was slightly tempered. Even so, the fire in his eyes was still plain enough to see.

Before Jeremiah could say anything else, the doors to the saloon busted open and another set of armed men came rushing inside. Unlike the previous group, however, these men were wearing badges.

"Oh for pity's sake, Jeremiah. What in the hell is going on here?" the man at the front of this new group asked.

Jeremiah shook his head. "Sheriff, I . . ."

"He was mistaken," Clint said. "That's all."

"And what about them?" the sheriff asked. When his eyes found the body on the floor, he added, "Or him?"

20

"Self-defense," Clint explained. "They had plenty of chances to avoid a fight and no reason to start shooting. They came at me with guns blazing and I did what I needed to do. Anyone here should be able to speak on my behalf."

Sheriff Hayes looked around at the scene in front of him. The saloon was a mess. There were overturned tables, chairs tossed all over the place and blood on the floor. Throughout the room, the people who'd taken cover before were now poking their heads out like prairie dogs testing for the sun.

"What do you say, Sal?" Hayes asked the barkeep. "Is he telling it the way it happened?"

The older man behind the bar seemed to be affected more by the damage he saw to the place and property than by the wounds of the three remaining gunmen. Finally, he looked over to the sheriff and nodded. "More or less. I didn't see everything, but that fella there didn't start anything."

"And who did?"

Immediately, Sal's eyes darted to Jeremiah and the shotgun he still held. Sal averted his gaze and shook his head. "Couldn't rightly say." Nodding toward the table where the gunmen had been playing their game, he added, "All I know for certain is that one of them four was the first to shoot."

Throughout the room, heads nodded in confirmation of what the barkeep said.

When the sheriff looked back to the wounded men, one of them caught his eye. The gunman who'd been shot in the leg had finally pulled himself over to his gun and was about to get a solid grip on the weapon. Hayes stepped over to that man, reached down and snatched the pistol from his hand.

"At least someone here is making my job easier," the sheriff said. "Jeremiah, hand over that shotgun."

Blinking rapidly, Jeremiah was assaulted by practically every one of his senses. There was the sight of bodies on the floor. The sound of gunfire still rang through his ears. Even his nostrils were filled, by the smell of black powder and blood.

Holding out his hand, Hayes said, "Jeremiah. You hear me?"

"Yeah," Jeremiah replied. "I hear you." He handed over the shotgun and used both hands to wipe away the sweat that had formed on his face.

Turning to Clint, Hayes said, "I know who you are. Clint Adams, right?"

"That's right."

"I've had my eye on these fellas here for a bit," the sheriff said, motioning toward the three remaining gunmen. "And since I don't see anyone saying any different, I'll have to go along with what you're telling me."

"I appreciate that, Sheriff," Clint said.

Hayes cocked his head and took another step forward. His deputies were sure to flank him protectively. "Even so," Hayes added while handing the shotgun to one of his men. "I'm going to need your gun. The judge is going to have to hear about this, since a man died here and all."

Clint looked over to Jeremiah and saw the man was turning pale and sweating profusely. Oddly enough, that was a good thing to see at that moment. He then drew the Colt in a slow, deliberate motion and handed it over to the sheriff.

"Will I be able to get that back?" Clint asked.

"After the trial goes your way, you'll get your property back. If it doesn't, well let's just say you'll have bigger concerns."

"I'm sure I will. Am I free to go?"

Nodding, Hayes said, "Sure. You're staying at the Mill House, right?"

"That's right."

"Just so long as I know where to find you." Hayes waited until Clint started to walk past him before adding,

"And one more thing, Adams. I guess you know that if you try to leave town without me knowing about it, I'll have to hunt you down and assume you're a dangerous fugitive."

"Yeah. I figured as much."

"Don't make me hunt you and put you down like a dog, Adams. I've heard you're a better man than that."

Looking over to the wounded gunmen that were being rounded up and hauled away by Hayes's deputies, Clint said, "That all depends on who you ask."

This time, Clint didn't ask if he could leave. No matter how much he wanted to stay in line with the law, going through those motions was starting to sit badly in the pit of his stomach. Clint didn't hold anything against a lawman trying to do his job. It was more the situation in general that was putting a sour taste in his mouth. He didn't like the thought of walking around town without a gun, but he didn't see any way out of handing it over unless he got tough with the sheriff, and he didn't want to do that. Besides, he had extra guns in his saddlebags.

When he stepped out of the saloon, Clint walked to the corner and pulled in a deep breath. The cold night air was like a splash of water in his face and went a long way to putting him into a better frame of mind. For a town of its size, Claymore's streets were still fairly crowded. Judging by the looks on the faces that passed Clint by and the speed in their steps, word about what had happened at Kylie's was spreading fast.

As much as Clint wanted to get back to his hotel room, he stood on that corner and soaked up some more of the cold air. Winter was on its way and the ground was already dusted with frost and a bit of snow that had fallen earlier that day. What little moonlight came from the pale sliver in the sky gave the streets a pale shimmer.

Of course, when Jeremiah Swann made his way out of Kylie's, that moonlight made his already pale skin look downright spooky. The big man stepped onto the boardwalk and looked around in a daze. He was pushed aside by the gunman with the wounded leg, who was being helped out by a pair of deputies.

The gunman barely got half a nudge in before he was pulled onto the street, but that was enough to stagger Jeremiah even more. Jeremiah reached out for the first post he could find to steady himself and then pulled in a few breaths to clear his own head.

When he saw Clint standing at the corner, Jeremiah walked straight toward him. If he'd been wearing a hat, it would have been in his hands. "Mister," Jeremiah said. "I don't have the words."

"Well, I can afford to wait," Clint replied. "It looks like I'll be in town for a while."

SEVEN

It was a cold night in Cheyenne. Although there had been a dusting of snow a few days ago, the flakes remained on the ground and stubbornly refused to melt no matter how many times the sun was able to break through the clouds. At night, the ground looked like rough, shining metal. Even the buildings took on a steely glint since the wood of their walls had frozen to a new hardness.

For people who lived in the area, this was nothing new. It was the time of year where the cold was getting colder and the days were getting shorter. It was a rough town in a rough part of the country. Even with all that under consideration, there were some people here who were rougher than others.

"You like that, bitch?" Sam Barkley grunted.

Sam's face was only partially illuminated by what little moonlight made it through his window, combined with the lantern that had been twisted down to something slightly more than a vague glow.

Sam was kneeling on his bed with his britches down around his ankles. His shirt hung open to expose a hairy belly that wobbled with every thrust of his hips. Muscled arms stretched down to not only hold himself up, but hold down the woman who was spread-eagled beneath him.

That woman was naked except for a thin camisole that clung to her body like a second skin. Firm, rounded breasts remained proud with nipples erect as she arched her back and opened her legs a bit more for Sam. Although her face was somewhat angular, there was a smoky sensuality in her eyes that was even more appealing when she responded to Sam's previous question.

"I like it, Sam," she breathed. "I like it even harder."

Sam's eyes widened and he licked his lips in anticipation. His cock grew even harder when he heard her talk that way. And when that happened, he felt the woman's slick pussy grasp him even tighter.

"You'll get it harder, Ally girl," Sam said. "You'll get it plenty harder."

Allison winced at the sound of her nickname coming from Sam's mouth. Not that he would notice, however, since she was keeping him plenty busy already.

Leaning back into the pillow, Allison closed her eyes and grabbed hold of Sam's arms. When she moved one leg up along his hips, she could feel every one of his thrusts from every angle. The muscles in his lower back tensed and relaxed as his rigid penis drove in and out of her with growing intensity.

With a little guidance from her leg as well as a little shifting of her hips against the mattress, Allison got herself settled just right so Sam could return some of the pleasure that she was giving to him. His cock started brushing against a spot inside of her that made her breath catch in her throat and her grip on him tighten.

"Oh, you like that, don't you?" Sam grunted. He reached up with both hands to cup her breasts, squeezing them in time to his thrusts. "You like that."

"Yes," Allison breathed. "Yes, yes."

For a moment, it seemed that she'd succeeded in training this man in record time. What had started as a clumsy advance and an awkward seduction was now becoming a night that might actually be a pleasant surprise for Allison. Sam responded well to her guidance, going where she wanted him to go while holding himself back long enough to do something while he was there.

As if sensing her thoughts, Sam started breathing more heavily and slamming into her even more. His hands were becoming rough on her breasts and his climax was beginning to show at the corners of his eyes and mouth.

Pulling in a breath, Allison grabbed hold of Sam's shoulders and pushed him back. Before he could say anything about it, she shifted her body while pushing him to one side. That brought him toppling to one side while she slid out from underneath him.

Sam was still trying to say something, but Allison was still moving both of them by the force of her own will. When they finally came to a stop, Sam was on his back and Allison was straddling him. Now Sam didn't seem so quick to protest as he'd been.

"Well now," Sam said with a leering grin. "Ain't this a nice little surprise."

He was looking up at Allison as she settled on top of him and found a comfortable spot. From this angle, he could make out the lines of her taut stomach muscles as well as the perfect way her breasts swayed when she moved. Her little nipples were even more erect now that she was where she wanted to be.

"You like that?" Allison asked, mocking the way Sam had been grunting moments before.

Whether Sam noticed her tone or not, he was in no position to protest. Her hands were running up and down over his chest. The camisole was twisted around her torso, outlining her curves as if it wasn't even there.

"Oh yeah, darlin'," Sam said. "I like this a lot."

Closing her eyes, Allison reached between her legs and quickly found Sam's rigid column of flesh. She guided it to the wet lips between her thighs and then settled down on top of it. Once she'd fully impaled herself, she opened her eyes and let out an easy breath.

"How about now?" she purred.

Just as Sam was starting to say something, his breath was taken away by the slow movements of Allison's hips. Although he started to pump his own hips in time to hers, he quickly found that she was doing just fine on her own. Once he lay back and gave in to her, the smile on Sam's face got even bigger.

Peeling open Sam's shirt, Allison leaned down and grabbed hold of his hands and thrust them above his head. All of her weight came down on them, effectively pinning him to the mattress. Not that he was going to resist, however, since her hips were still rocking back and forth. Her tight pussy massaged every inch of him in its silky embrace.

It seemed that Allison was about to say something, but this time it was *her* breath that was taken away. While leaning forward, she'd managed to press herself against his erection so that she quickly found herself spiraling toward an orgasm.

The more pleasure she felt, the more urgently she rode him. Her hands clenched tightly around Sam's and she lowered herself down until every inch of his cock was buried inside of her. From there, she started pumping her hips quickly back and forth.

As the bed started creaking noisily beneath them, Allison started moaning louder and louder. Her heart slammed in her chest and sweat started soaking into the tight cotton camisole twisted around her body.

When Sam looked up at her, he did so with wide, almost disbelieving eyes. While he'd been close to his own climax earlier, she'd set him back a little ways when she'd taken such rough control of him. After that, he found himself feeling so good that he started to wonder if he was dreaming this whole night.

In a few moments, Sam felt Allison's body start to shudder. Her face was intent on what she was doing and her eyes were clenched tightly shut. Even after she let go of one of his hands, Sam kept his arm up over his head so he wouldn't break whatever spell she was under.

Allison snapped her head back, flipping her long blond hair over her shoulders. While letting out a soft groan, she straightened her back until she seemed to be looking down from a mile on top of him. With her spine straight, she kept her hips grinding back and forth.

One of her hands wandered over Sam's stomach, teasing the spot between his legs where he was entering her. A sly grin came onto Allison's face, which quickly became intense with a sudden jolt of pleasure.

Allison's climax was taking her over. When it washed through her body, it tightened her pussy around his cock, while sending a shudder up her back that caused her back to arch until she was staring up at the rafters in the ceiling.

Her mouth came open, but no sound came out. Taking in that sight, Sam was pushed back to where he'd been a few moments ago. His chest and stomach were moist with the sweat Allison had worked up, and the entire room smelled like the sweet musk of her skin and hair.

Even after her breaths had slowed and her chest had stopped heaving, Allison continued to ride Sam's cock in a slow, luxurious grind that caused Sam to close his eyes and let out a series of building groans.

Just as he was about to explode inside of her, Sam opened his eyes to get another look at Allison's tight, muscular body. Although her camisole was still clinging to her perfectly and her nipples were erect beneath the cotton, none of that was what caught Sam's attention.

Instead, his eyes were drawn to the Derringer clutched in her hand.

EIGHT

"What the hell?" Sam asked breathlessly.

Pressing the pistol up under Sam's chin, Allison leaned down so she could stare directly into his eyes. His cock was still rigid inside of her, and she didn't seem to mind it one bit. In fact, there was more excitement in her eyes now than when she'd first felt his hands upon her skin.

"Shut your mouth for a second," Allison demanded.

It felt good for her to speak what was on her mind for a change. After allowing herself to be pushed around by the brutish cowboy under her, turning the tables was the biggest sexual rush she'd felt in a while.

Allison's finger tensed around the Derringer's trigger as she rubbed her hips against him.

Laying flat on his back with that gun under his chin, Sam was torn between two extremes. On one hand, Allison was riding him expertly and seemed intent on bringing him to an orgasm while bringing herself there at least one more time. On the other hand, every twitch in her body, whether it came from pleasure or anything else, caused that trigger to be pulled back another fraction of an inch.

Sam's body ached to release between Allison's taut thighs while his brain waited to hear the pop and feel the bullet drill up through his skull.

"Mmm," Allison purred. "This is the best part." Opening her eyes all the way, she put on a wicked smile and asked, "What about you? You like that, bitch?"

"Wh-what's going on here?" Sam demanded as his pleasure was forced upon him.

"Just relax for a moment," she insisted. "There's plenty of time for the rest."

Before Sam could say anything else, he felt Allison's muscles clench around the base of his cock. She wriggled her hips and rode him in short thrusts. Soon, Sam's breaths were growing short and he felt his orgasm coming on its own accord.

As the pleasure swept through him and finally exploded, he couldn't help but feel better. He figured she might just be teasing him or playing some sort of game. But when he saw her let out the last of her own moaning breaths, he knew she wasn't playing.

"There," she whispered. "Now we can talk." When she felt Sam start to move a little too much beneath her, she pushed the Derringer up a little harder under his chin. "No you don't. Just lay there and let me do the work."

Although he was already spent, Sam couldn't deny that having Allison where she was felt good. She could have been holding a shotgun to his forehead and the warmth of her body against his would still have been good. Even so, he knew that feeling would change real quick with just a little tug from one of her fingers.

"You know who I am?" Allison asked.

Sam's brow crinkled and he paused for a moment before answering. "Sure I know who you are. I been fuckin' you haven't I?"

Smiling at his crude words, Allison nodded. "You think

you're the one that's been running things tonight? That's sweet."

"What the hell do you want? You were all over me just like I was on you, so you can't complain about what went on here."

"No. I wasn't going to complain. Actually, you weren't too bad. You weren't too good, but—"

"I've had enough of this," Sam snarled. "Get that little popgun out of my face."

"You'd better watch your tongue, Sammy. Or this pop-gun of mine will pop a bullet right into your brain."

Gritting his teeth, Sam weighed his options and couldn't come up with any that seemed to tip in his favor.

Once she saw the resignation fall onto him, Allison straightened up a bit. "Now, apart from the woman who acted like you had more charm than a hungry mutt begging for table scraps, do you know who I am?"

Considering what his answer would be, Sam figured it was in his best interest to just keep his mouth shut.

"How about I tell you who I am? My name is Allison Little. Sound familiar?"

Sam's face remained still and petulant. When he felt the Derringer jab against his jaw one more time, he spat out, "No."

"How about Jamie Little? Does that ring any bells?"

Sam kept quiet, allowing his brain to try and figure a way out of this unexpected mess.

"Jamie Little from Wichita," Allison added.

That caused Sam's heart to skip a beat and his eyes to widen enough for Allison to notice.

Nodding slowly, she said, "I thought that might strike a chord or two."

"I didn't have nothing to do with what happened to her," Sam said. "I wasn't even there when it happened."

"You mean when she died," Allison corrected. "Or better yet, when she was murdered." She pulled in a breath, held it and let it out in a barely controlled stream. As the air escaped her lungs, it left her eyes cold and her face a stony mask.

"She was a good little girl and was becoming a fine woman," Allison said. "She was quiet as a mouse and would never harm another living thing. I used to be like that, myself. That is, until my good, kind sister was slaughtered like livestock."

"What do you want from me?" Sam gasped. He was frightened by the shadow that had come over her and wasn't even trying to hide it. "I told you I wasn't there that night."

"But your friend was. I want to know where he is."

"He couldn't have killed her, either."

"Don't," she said, thumbing back the hammer and twisting the Derringer slightly against Sam's jaw. "Just . . . don't."

"I rode through hell and back with that man. He saved my life in th—"

"I know all that. Why do you think I let you put your hands on me so I could get you here instead of just talking to you like a civilized person? You're a big talker, Sammy, but you're not that tough. Look at you now. Your prick's just a limp noodle now that you're away from your gun."

"I'll tell you what you want to know. I'll tell you anything."

"Yeah," Allison whispered. "You sure as hell will."

NINE

Clint had plenty he wanted to say to Jeremiah Swann. There were questions that needed to be asked and plenty for the man to explain. But rather than try to have that conversation when both of them were still reeling from getting shot at, Clint decided to let the other man off the hook so the blood could cool a bit in his veins.

Also, Clint had been playing his game of poker for close to twelve hours before it had been busted up. The chips had come and gone, but it looked as though he was meant to break even that night. Without something drastic happening, Clint had been having a good enough time that he might very well have still been there if Jeremiah had picked another place to start his rampage.

By the time he got back to his rented room, Clint was glad he and Jeremiah had simply parted ways. All he had to do was look at his bed and his eyelids felt like they were weighted down with lead sinkers. He opened his saddlebags and extracted the little .32 Colt New Line that he used as a hideout gun. He put it under his pillow, then managed to peel off his shirt, his hat, his gun belt and one boot before dropping onto the mattress and passing out.

• • •

The next morning, Clint rolled out of bed and stretched his arms. For a moment, with the sun beaming in through his window and warming his face, it seemed that the previous night might have been a restless dream. All he needed to do was smell the black powder on his hands to dispel that feeling.

"Damn," Clint whispered to himself. "Looks like I'm really stuck in Claymore."

Not that the town was all that bad. As far as towns went, Claymore had enough to keep anyone content for a while. There was even a theater in town, along with enough poker games to keep Clint busy for weeks on end.

The previous morning, Clint had been considering staying on for a while longer anyhow. But getting an order to stay put appealed to the contrary nature of any man. Clint was no exception. The moment the sheriff told him he couldn't leave town, Clint wanted to saddle up Eclipse and ride away.

He shook his head and chuckled under his breath. He guessed that if Hayes had told him to get the hell out of Claymore, Clint would be waking up this morning wanting to take in a show or have another drink at Kylie's. Nothing like a good laugh to start the day.

After changing his clothes and splashing some water onto his face, Clint was feeling much better. All he needed was some breakfast and a hot cup of coffee and he might even be better. When he buckled the holster around his waist, he took a moment to pause.

The weight of the pistol was as familiar as the weight of his own arms hanging from his shoulders. Waking up with that weight missing was like having to pin up his sleeve for the first time after losing an arm. He stood in his spot, wondering for a moment if he should wear the gun belt or not.

Shaking his head, he unbuckled the belt and tossed it onto his bed.

• • •

Hearing the sound of footsteps coming down the stairs on the other side of the room, the old woman behind the hotel's front desk turned to take a look in that direction. When she saw the familiar face, she quickly searched through a short stack of paper and then held up a slip triumphantly.

"Mr. Adams," the old woman said quickly. "Over here."

Clint turned toward the eager voice, still feeling a bit naked without the gun belt around his waist. "Good morning."

Returning Clint's smile, the old woman looked as though she was out of breath. Her hair was silvery gray, but was still kept long and hung down past her shoulders. She wore a dark blue dress which rustled against the edge of the desk as she came around it.

"Good morning, Mr. Adams. There's a message for you."

Clint's stomach dropped a bit when he guessed at who would want to leave him a message. More than likely, it was from Sheriff Hayes. It could also have been from one of the gunmen or one of their friends, looking to even a score.

Rather than let his imagination run wild, Clint held out his hand and asked, "A message? Do you know who it's from?"

When the old woman paused, it sent an unwelcome chill down Clint's spine.

Finally, she lowered her voice and said, "It's from Jeremiah Swann."

"Oh," Clint said, feeling some of the tension leave him.

"That poor man. Do you know what happened to his daughter?"

"Not specifically. I know she was killed, but nothing more than that."

The old woman winced. She looked around and didn't speak again until she was certain there wasn't anyone else close enough to listen. "She was found propped up just outside of town."

"Propped up?"

"Plain as day, just like she was sitting out there enjoying the weather. Plenty of people saw her. I think I might have even seen her there, but nobody thought anything of it."

"And she was left there, dead?"

"Not just dead," she whispered, lowering her head as though she expected to feel a sting on the back of her neck. "She was murdered. I heard that she was hurt so bad that the poor girl must have fallen into the hands of some savages."

"What?"

"Savages," she repeated. "She was scalped."

"Good lord," Clint whispered. Looking down at the note in his hands, he thought back to the last time he'd seen the man who'd written it. In fact, after hearing this, he wasn't too surprised at the crazy fire that had been in Jeremiah's eyes the night before.

"That poor man," the old woman said. "Give him my best."

But Clint was already walking through the front door. He acknowledged the woman's request with a quick nod.

TEN

The note left for Clint was short and written in a rough scrawl that was difficult to read. It was a simple request for him to come to Jeremiah's shop at the corner of Eighth and Main.

Since he'd spent a bit of time in Claymore, there was no problem finding his way to Jeremiah's shop. In fact, before he got there, Clint could hear the clanging of steel on steel. The sharp sound fell in a smooth, easy rhythm that started to sound like a code.

Clang . . . clang . . . clang-clang.

Clang . . . clang . . . clang-clang.

By the time Clint was close enough to see Jeremiah stooped over his anvil, his steps were falling into the rhythm of the blacksmith's hammer.

Jeremiah's shop was on the eastern edge of town. It looked like most other blacksmith's shops, complete with a medium-sized shed and a larger area outside covered by a wooden awning. Beneath the awning, there was the anvil, several buckets of water, a long table and a few racks of tools. The forge glowed red not too far from Jeremiah's side, giving his features even more intensity than they already had.

Jeremiah Swann was even more imposing in his ele-

ment than when he'd been storming through Kylie's with a
shotgun in his hands. The big man was wrapped up in a
thick, battered apron and had his shirtsleeves rolled up to
reveal thick, muscled arms.

When he lifted the hammer, he did so as if the heavy
tool was nothing more than a twig. Swinging it down, he
connected against the metal he was working to send out a
spray of sparks. After a few more strikes, Jeremiah moved
the hot metal from the anvil with a large pair of tongs and
dipped it into the closest bucket of water. Steam hissed
loudly as he swirled the metal inside the bucket.

"Mornin', Adams," Jeremiah said. "You got my note?"

"That's why I'm here."

"Yeah. I suppose so. Just a minute, all right?"

"Sure. Take your time."

Actually, Jeremiah only needed another minute or so
before he was able to set aside what he was working on and
put down his tools. He walked over to Clint, brushing his
hands against the front of his apron. "Glad you could make
it, Adams," he said, extending a blackened, beefy hand. "I
appreciate it."

Clint shook the blacksmith's hand, which was almost as
rough and hot as the iron of the anvil itself. "I heard about
what happened to your daughter. I'm sorry."

Jeremiah's eyes didn't twitch. In fact, he seemed to have
grown colder and more callous in the hours since they'd
last talked. "Did you have anything to do with it?"

"Well, no."

"Then you don't need to be sorry. I'm the one that
should apologize to you. I would've last night, but—"

"Forget about it," Clint interrupted. "Water under the
bridge."

This time, Jeremiah did flinch. It was a barely percepti-
ble twitch, but it told Clint a lot. For Jeremiah Swann, there
wasn't a bridge built just yet that could get him through
this flood.

"I wanted to talk to you to make sure you knew I didn't mean to hurt anyone last night," Jeremiah said.

Clint's eyes narrowed as he walked over to the forge so he could warm his hands. "Really? Turning a shotgun on a crowded saloon is a funny way to go about not hurting anyone."

"The men I was after ain't even human. Anyone that could do that to my little girl ain't nothing more than a rabid dog. Killing that son of a bitch ain't murder. It's putting down something that needs to be dead."

"But it would sure have helped if you knew exactly who you were after. To be honest, I don't even think those gunhands were a part of what happened to your daughter."

"Well, they sure as hell started shooting quick enough."

"Men like that are always itching for a fight. And having you stroll in the way you did was more than enough to light that fuse."

The blacksmith nodded. "I guess you're right about that, too."

"Sheriff Hayes seems like he knows what he's doing. Why don't you mourn your little girl and let the law do its job? I doubt she'd want her father getting himself killed because he stepped into a hornet's nest which he could just as easily have avoided."

"Actually, that's what I wanted to talk to you about, Mr. Adams."

"You want to make sure you stay out of another fight?"

"No. Not quite."

ELEVEN

The shack that held up the awning over Jeremiah's forge seemed even smaller once the blacksmith stepped into it. Clint followed him in and had to watch his step to make sure that he didn't trip over some spare piece of iron or a misplaced tool.

"Watch yourself," Jeremiah muttered. "My Mary usually cleans up once a week in here. I guess I should start doing that myself now."

"It's all right," Clint said as he found a place to sit. "I'll manage. So will you once this has a chance to settle."

Jeremiah lowered himself down onto the edge of a thick counter which was covered with scraps of metal, wood and even a few broken tools. Crossing his arms over his chest, he took a moment before looking up and fixing his eyes upon Clint.

"You have any kids, Adams?"

"I've never raised any, no."

"Have you ever lost a child or even lost someone who was that close to you?"

Clint knew where the conversation was headed. He also knew better than to try and work his way through it. "I've

42

lost plenty of people I cared about," Clint said evenly. "But I won't pretend to know what you're going through."

"Good. 'Cause there's no way in hell you could ever know how I feel after finding my sweet girl torn apart like she wasn't nothing but meat."

"Whoever did that won't get away with it, Jeremiah. The law's on their trail and isn't about to let killers like that get a moment's rest before they pay for what they've done."

"Can you guarantee that?" Jeremiah asked. "Can you look me in the eyes and tell me that my girl's death will be avenged?"

Clint did look into Jeremiah's eyes, and he did so without faltering in the slightest. "If it's vengeance you're after, then you'll never feel that fire in your belly go away."

For a moment, Jeremiah seemed ready to jump across the room and put Clint through a wall. Before he did anything so drastic, he let out the breath he'd been holding and shifted his gaze toward the floor. "You sound like you're talking from experience, Adams."

"I've seen enough blood spilled for the wrong reasons to know what I'm talking about. I've also seen men ruin their lives chasing after something that will work its way toward the people who deserve it without any help at all."

"I've got no doubt that the animals who killed my Mary will burn for what they done," Jeremiah said. "My only worry is that some more innocent blood will be spilled before that happens."

Clint studied the blacksmith's face. Something had shifted beneath the man's eyes. It was still anger, to be certain, but there was more focus to it than before. "What makes you say that?" Clint asked. "What have you heard?"

Jeremiah's eyes snapped back toward Clint. "Let's just say that my Mary isn't the first girl to be killed like this."

"That's not exactly news."

"Not just the scalping," Jeremiah said through gritted teeth. "The way Mary was propped up out in the open. The way she was set to look so peaceful. Other girls were killed like that. Other girls the same age as Mary. They even looked a bit like her, from what I hear."

"Where have you heard this, Jeremiah?" Clint put a fire of his own into his gaze as he said, "Look, you wanted me to meet you and here I am. You wanted to talk to me, so I'm listening. You obviously have more to say, so just say it."

"The law ain't going to find the killer that's out there," the blacksmith said bluntly. "They're not even on the right path."

"What makes you so sure about that?"

"They're looking for an Indian, first off. Either that, or some other mad dog killer living out in the wild."

"You know that for a fact?"

Jeremiah nodded. "Talked to Sheriff Hayes this morning. Heard him say them words myself."

"And you think he's headed in the wrong direction?"

"I'm no expert, but it just don't make sense to me. Have you ever heard of an Injun scalping some girl and then leaving her out there for all the world to see?"

Truth be told, Clint hadn't heard of Indians scalping half as many people as the stories about them suggested. Scalping in general wasn't even started by the Indians. It was used mostly by the people who hunted Indians down as a way of tallying up their kills when they went in to collect their pay.

Running all of that through his head, Clint replied, "No. I've never really heard of that."

"And that don't even make sense, does it?"

"Anyone who would do a thing like this isn't going to make a whole lot of sense."

"I know, I know. But something in my gut tells me that Sheriff Hayes is going about this all wrong."

"Then maybe you should tell him that."

"Already did," Jeremiah said.

"What did he say?"

"That I should go about my life and try to get over what happened. He damn near patted me on my head and sent me on my way, for Christ's sake."

Trying to sound as earnest as he could without adding fuel to Jeremiah's fire, Clint said, "That might not be a bad idea, you know. After something like this happens, you need to move on."

"I can't. No man would in my place, either."

"I know, but you almost got yourself killed in that saloon last night. If you go after more dangerous men looking for the right one, you're going to be kicking up a storm that'll be too big for anyone to pull you out."

Jeremiah nodded. "You're right about that, which is why I need someone to help me do what needs to be done. I can't do this on my own, Mr. Adams. That much I know for certain. But whoever did this is gonna hurt someone else. I know that as well."

As much as Clint wanted to talk some sense into the blacksmith, he couldn't deny the fact that Jeremiah was already making plenty of sense. "Maybe I should talk to the law about this," Clint offered. "Perhaps the sheriff will listen to someone else."

"The law won't do you no good," came a voice from the doorway leading to the workspace outside the shack.

Clint and Jeremiah turned in that direction with a start. Neither man had heard anyone approaching. When they got a look at who was in the doorway, they were surprised yet again.

The woman who stood there filled out a good portion of the opening. While she was tall for a lady, she had ahold of the frame with both hands in a loose grip that was imposing and seductive at the same time. Long, dark blond hair was tied at the back of her head in a braid that was hanging down the front of one shoulder. She wore jeans, a thick cotton shirt and a beaten leather jacket that appeared to have weathered more storms than the body they covered.

"Sorry to interrupt," she said, "but Mr. Swann is right. The law's got their sights set for an Indian, which will just let the animal who killed his daughter kill again. And make no mistake about it, he will kill again."

TWELVE

Clint took in the sight of the blonde standing in the doorway. Even though her arrival was a surprise, she seemed to belong right where she was standing. Stepping toward her, Clint said, "You seem to know what you're talking about, Miss . . ."

"Oh," she said as if she suddenly realized where she was and what she was doing. "It's Allison Little." Extending her hand, she added, "But just Allison is fine. Miss just doesn't fit me too well."

"All right then, Allison," Clint said while shaking her hand. "I'd introduce myself as well, but you seem to know who we are well enough."

"I know he's Jeremiah Swann," she said, pointing toward the bigger of the two men in the room. Shifting her eyes back in Clint's direction, she said, "I've got a notion about you, but I'm not so sure."

"I'm Clint Adams."

"And here I thought it was just a rumor that you were in town. So many loudmouths try to pass themselves off as a known man when they get into a scrape that it hardly pays to take any notice of it."

"Now that we've got the formalities out of the way,"

47

Clint said, "how about you tell us just what you're doing here and why you're barging into a private conversation?"

Jeremiah nodded. "I'd like to know that myself."

"I just got into town and I was hoping to talk to someone who might be able to give me some information."

"You seem pretty well informed already."

"True enough, Mr. Adams, but there's still plenty more I need to find out. First off, I'd like to talk to Mr. Swann about his daughter."

"I don't even know you," Jeremiah said with growing anger in his voice. "Why should I tell you a damned thing? How do you even know about me? How'd you recognize me, anyway?"

"Well," she said with a shrug, "for starters, I knew I needed to look for the town's blacksmith, and you're the only one here wearing a blacksmith's apron."

Jeremiah looked down at his apron. When he looked back up again, he seemed a little embarrassed. "That still don't explain what you're doing here."

"Give her a chance, Jeremiah," Clint said, trying to calm the blacksmith before he got too worked up. "I think she was just about to tell us that on her own. Weren't you, Allison?"

She stepped into the shack, while pulling the door shut behind her. Although she didn't exactly push Clint back, she moved with such certainty that she left little doubt in anyone's mind that she didn't mean to let anyone stop her.

When she got closer, Clint couldn't help but feel the heat off her body and the familiar way she brushed against him.

"I'd very much like to talk to you, Mr. Swann," she said once the door was shut and the latch had dropped. "With all due respect, I'd first like to make sure that Mr. Adams is here on the same business I am."

"We don't know what your business is, lady," Jeremiah said.

"I heard about your daughter," she replied in a somber tone.

Clint didn't like the sound of that one bit. "Hold on, now. Are you from around here?"

"No."

"I didn't think so. How could you have heard about his daughter? It barely happened a day ago."

"Let's just say that the animal that killed her isn't new to what he does. He's done it plenty of times before, and I've been trying to track him down long enough to know what to look for. I got lucky in this case because I've got some friends who live here in town and they sent me a telegram letting me know what happened."

"Who are these friends?" Clint asked. "What did they tell you?"

Allison seemed torn. Although it looked like she wanted to answer him, there was something preventing her from doing so. "Maybe I should just talk to Mr. Swann alone?"

"That's up to him," Clint replied.

Shaking his head more out of frustration than anything else, Jeremiah threw up his hands and said, "if it'll get this woman out of here so I can keep doing the work I need to do, then it's fine with me."

Allison stepped past Clint until she could get a good look straight into Jeremiah's eyes. "It won't take long for you to see that we're both in the middle of the same job."

"And that job requires you to walk around armed?" Clint asked.

Both Allison and Jeremiah seemed surprised by that.

Quickly, Jeremiah reached out and slapped open one of the flaps of her jacket. When he saw the gun belt strapped around her waist, he shook his head. Without the slightest pause, he reached over and took hold of what appeared to be a botched attempt at a branding iron.

"You got three seconds to explain yerself, miss," Jeremiah said.

Without taking her eyes from the iron in Jeremiah's hands, she said, "Clint, you can take my gun from me if you want. It's important that I talk to him about this right here and right now. I rode all the way from Cheyenne to get here and I'm not about to be turned away."

"Sounds fair," Clint said as he leaned forward and plucked the gun from Allison's holster. Holding the weapon so Jeremiah could see it, he added, "Couldn't hurt to hear her out."

"I guess not. Check back with me in half an hour." Looking to Allison, Jeremiah asked, "Will that be enough time?"

She ignored the sarcasm in his voice and nodded. "Plenty. I truly appreciate this. Both of you."

"All right then. Maybe I can get some breakfast."

When Clint stepped outside, he took a look at the gun for himself. All in all, it was a fine weapon. The balance was good, the sights had been filed down and the trigger guard had been removed. It was a gun meant for someone fairly good at firing one.

He flipped open the cylinder to find it was fully loaded. Fitting the gun under his belt, he pulled his jacket over it. He'd give Allison her time alone, but he decided not to stray too far from the blacksmith's shop after all.

THIRTEEN

Fifteen minutes later, the door leading into the blacksmith's shack swung open and Allison stepped out. She was quickly followed by Jeremiah, who went straight to his tools and got to work. The look in his eyes made Clint wonder if the bigger man even saw much of anything at all.

Allison spotted Clint standing across the street and headed straight for him. When she got close enough, she held out her hand and said, "As you can see, he's unharmed. Can I have my gun back now?"

"Sure," Clint said. He carefully removed the firearm from where it was stored and handed it back to its owner. "Has that always been yours?"

She gave him a sideways glance as she took her gun back. "That's an odd question."

"And that's a serious weapon. It's got some modifications that usually only gunfighters worry about."

"It's mine," she said with a smirk. "And who's to say that I'm not a gunfighter?"

"That would explain why you knew I'd be in town as though an advertisement had been posted."

Rather than answer him right away, Allison gave Clint a

lingering smile. "Did you have your breakfast yet, or were you waiting outside this whole time?"

"I was waiting outside."

"Great, because I'm starving. Care to join me?"

"Sure. Why not?"

They walked up to the corner and then made their way to Sixth Street without another word passing between them. Finally, Allison started to laugh under her breath.

"What's so funny?" Clint asked.

"Nothing. That was cute, is all."

"What was?"

"The way you acted as if you actually had to think about joining me for breakfast."

"Was it so obvious that I'm so hungry I could eat a piece of leather?"

"No," Allison replied. "It was more obvious that you had no intention of letting me out of your sight until you got a chance to rake me over the coals for a while."

Rather than try to dance around her statement, Clint asked, "Can you blame me?"

She thought about that for a few seconds, making it perfectly obvious that she really didn't need to think about it at all. "I guess not."

They walked for a little ways before falling into a growing stream of people which seemed to be headed mostly in one direction. From there, all they needed to do was allow themselves to be swept into the flow of movement and they soon found themselves standing right where they needed to be.

The place was a small restaurant that Clint had been to several times already. No matter what time of day it was, the air inside the modest building always smelled like breakfast. There wasn't much to choose from as far as open tables went, but they were shown to a little round one in the back.

"It's all we have left," said the young man who'd shown them to their place. "Sorry."

"No need for that," Allison said. "This'll be just fine with me."

After sitting down and allowing a cup of coffee to be poured for him, Clint waited until the server walked away before saying, "Somehow I got the notion you'd prefer it back here."

"And you wouldn't?" she shot back. "I see that you somehow managed to put your back to a wall just as I did."

Clint actually looked behind him to confirm her accusation. "Old habits," he said with a shrug.

She lifted her coffee as if to toast him. "They're not the only things that die hard."

The brew was strong and rich, coating Clint's throat as it went down. Although it tasted as if it could have come from the bottom of a long-brewing pot, it was more than enough to put a little more steam in Clint's belly.

"I don't suppose you'll tell me what you and Jeremiah discussed while you two were alone?" Clint asked.

She smiled and shook her head while sipping from her own cup. "Maybe you should ask him. If he'd like you to know about it, then he can tell you."

"Fair enough. Then let's have a conversation of our own."

"You do like to cut through things, Clint. I like that in a man."

"What are you doing in Claymore?" he asked directly. "And what have you got to do with whoever killed Jeremiah's daughter?"

Although her manner still seemed pleasant enough, a shadow came over her that had strictly to do with a darkness from inside herself. She weighed some options in her head, picked one and then let out a breath to follow it through.

"I come from a small family in Wichita," she said. "I won't bore you with needless details, but I'll have you know that I loved my family very much and we had a good, simple, clean life.

"That all came to a stop one night almost two years ago. My sister Jamie was thirteen and she was giving my parents grief over something or other the way thirteen-year-olds do. I woke up and found that she was gone. We all thought she'd run away and would come back when she got cold and hungry enough to see reason again."

Allison took a deep breath and lowered her head until she appeared to be studying the wisps of steam rising from her coffee cup. Without looking up, she said, "I found her sitting at the edge of our property, looking pretty as you please in her favorite dress. Her hair was wet and it looked like she was just about to talk to me.

"When I got closer, I saw she wasn't moving. When I tried to move her, she dropped over and part of her hair peeled back like one of those old powdered wigs." She stopped there and looked up. Although her strength had returned, it was steely and cold. "I've been looking for the animal that killed her ever since."

Clint didn't know what to say. No matter how many times he'd stared death in the face, it was always easier than having to comfort someone after they or someone close to them had lost that same battle. But this was something different.

This was death for death's sake, and it sent a chill down Clint's spine that he rarely felt anymore.

"I-I'm sorry," Clint said, even as he shrugged as if to apologize for the apology.

Allison thought back to those demons before pushing them away with a quick shake of her head. "I'm past all that now."

"Are you?"

"The consoling, the mourning, the fear. It's all behind me."

"What about the anger?"

"That?" she asked. Soon, she shook her head. "Not quite yet. But I am seeing straight enough to know I'll get some peace once this killer is put into the ground. I don't know how many times he's killed before my sister or since, but Jeremiah's daughter is proof that it won't just stop on its own.

"And don't bother telling me to stop," she continued. "I've already heard the speeches about vengeance as well as all the useless talk about sitting back to let the law run its course."

"Actually, I wasn't going to say any of that," Clint told her.

"Really? What were you about to say?"

"I was just going to tell you to leave Jeremiah out of this. He's got plenty to worry about without being pulled onto your warpath."

FOURTEEN

The road leading into Claymore was rutted and well traveled. It was like a major blood vessel leading into the heart of town. For the moment, however, the heart didn't seem to be beating and no blood was running through the vein.

A group of men and their horses stood gathered at a specific spot on the road like a clot. They clustered together, and while they didn't move as a group, each one of them was moving slowly on his own. Standing at the center of the group was Sheriff Hayes. His deputies spread out from him with their hands stuffed in their pockets and their eyes fixed on the ground.

"Don't move too quickly," the sheriff said. "And for God's sake watch where you're stepping before you put your feet down."

While he wasn't the oldest of the deputies, one of them in particular carried himself with more authority. In fact, he was the one who never strayed more than five or six feet from the sheriff's side. "Are you sure we can—"

The deputy's question was cut short by a quick, stern glare from Hayes.

Lowering his voice and taking a careful step closer to the sheriff, the deputy leaned in and spoke again. "Are you sure we can find anything out here, Sheriff? I mean, there must be a hundred sets of tracks on this road."

"We might not find any tracks," Hayes replied. "But we can find something."

"Like what?"

Although the sheriff wanted to shoot an answer straight back to the deputy, he stopped before letting out the breath he'd just taken. Finally, he let it out and shook his head. "Hell, Chapman, I don't know."

Despite the fact that the sheriff's voice was barely more than a whisper, a few of the other deputies looked up from where they were searching. They then looked around at each other with doubt spreading over their faces.

Sheriff Hayes looked down at a spot not too far from where he was standing. The stump was sticking out of the ground like a single tooth in an otherwise barren mouth. On the stump, as well as on the ground nearby, there were dark red stains from blood that had become almost black since it had been spilled from Mary Swann's body.

"There's got to be something here," Hayes muttered.

Chapman was in his late twenties. His lean frame was covered in dark clothes, with his deputy badge displayed prominently on his chest. The gun he wore was carried low without being put on display. His face was a little too grim for someone his age and lightly dusted with a thin beard.

All in all, Chapman wasn't the type of man to blindly follow orders. While the rest of the deputies scrounged in the dirt for tracks they knew they weren't about to find, Chapman was already setting his sights for something else.

Although such qualities were to be admired at some times, this was not one of those times.

"You got something else to say?" Hayes snapped as he caught Chapman staring in another direction. "Or maybe you've got somewhere else to be?"

"Did you know Mary Swann?" the deputy asked.

The question seemed to catch Hayes off his guard.

While the anger was still frozen onto his face, it wasn't as intense as it had previously been. "Not particularly."

"I did. She was a sweet, smart girl."

"What's your point?"

"My point is that she was too smart to wander off into some Indian camp or pester some group of savages passing through. And she was too sweet to have an enemy in the world."

Placing his hands upon his hips and standing toe to toe with Chapman, the sheriff stared directly into his deputy's face. "She could have been the most cherished, smartest girl in this county, but that still wouldn't make her strong enough to fight off some redskin who wanted to scalp her."

"Why would they do that, though?" Chapman asked. "We haven't had a problem with the redskins for . . . I don't even know how long."

"And that's how I aim to keep it, Chapman." Shifting his eyes so he could address each of his men in turn, Sheriff Hayes spoke in a slow, snarling voice. "We're dealing with an animal here. It's not like anything you men have ever seen. Hell, it's not like anything I've ever seen. But I do know that animals don't think like men. That's what makes them dangerous."

Once again, Hayes turned so that he was talking to Chapman alone. His voice remained raised so anyone in the vicinity could hear when he asked, "You understand me, or should I say it clearer?"

Chapman didn't back down. Although he kept a respectful tone, he didn't allow himself to be cowed by the senior lawman. "I understand. It's just that we're still standing here looking at nothing when whoever did this could have gotten off to just about anywh—"

"Sheriff!" came a voice from a few yards away. "I think I might've found something."

Everyone turned to look at the man who'd broken in on the other two. They found one of the other deputies, a squat man with long brown hair, bending at the knees and squinting at a spot on the ground in front of him.

"What is it, Dell?" Hayes asked.

"I ain't quite sure," the other deputy said. "But I think it's gotta be something."

Hayes and Chapman looked at each other in a way that was bordering on a stare-down. Although there was some aggression in both men's eyes, none of it seemed to be directed at one another just yet. After a respectable amount of time, Hayes broke away from the clash to see what had captured Dell's attention.

The squat deputy now had his hands pressed flat against his knees so he could hunker down and get a look at something on the ground. When he saw the sheriff approach, he took half a shuffling step aside and pointed at the cold dirt.

"Look there," Dell said. "You see it?"

Hayes didn't see anything at first. All Dell was pointing at was the rough ground at the side of the road. There was some dirt and plenty of rocks that had been kicked to the side from countless passing horses and wagons, but not much else.

Hunkering down a bit himself, Hayes focused his tired eyes even harder on the spot where Dell was pointing. He could see some more gravel as well as some crusted remains of dead leaves. There was also a thick root protruding from the ground like the back of some thick, petrified worm. His eyes ran along the length of the root just so he could satisfy himself that it indeed led back to the stump where Mary's body had been found.

Just as he was about to ask Dell what on earth had gotten him so riled up, Hayes stopped and peered in even closer. "What the hell?"

"You see it, don't you?" Dell asked.

Something had been carved into the side of the root. It was a rough figure made up of short, straight cuts from a sharp blade. "Yeah, I see it."

"Looks like it had to be pretty recent. The inside of the cuts ain't even turned color yet."

Chapman had come over to get a look for himself. Although he couldn't get as close as he'd like without pushing the other two aside, he'd spotted something else. "Look here," he said. "Tracks. And these aren't like the others."

"How so?" Hayes asked while looking back over his shoulder.

"There ain't no heel prints. And they look more rounded than any boot I ever seen."

"That's because they weren't made by boots."

"More like moccasins," Chapman said.

Hayes and all the other deputies there started to nod. Then they looked back to the sheriff with renewed determination.

The blood rushed a bit faster in Hayes's veins. Now that he knew the time spent looking around this spot hadn't been wasted, his thoughts were moving faster than ever. "You see any more of them prints, Chapman?"

"Sure do."

"Then scout ahead and see where they lead."

"Yes, sir," Chapman said.

Leaning over the sheriff's shoulder, Dell kept his eyes on the root he'd found and asked, "You think that's an Indian carving?"

"I don't know what it is, but it's something we didn't have before. Fetch Ernie Niedelander and have him look at this. The rest of you get ready to ride. We've got some tracks to follow."

FIFTEEN

"Not that I'm complaining," Allison said as she poured some syrup onto her griddle cakes, "but what brings about this loyalty for the blacksmith? Is he an old friend of yours?"

Clint shrugged before biting into the thick strip of bacon that had come with his own breakfast. "He's a good man who's too close to getting his life more ruined than it already is. Let him deal with his ghosts his own way and you deal with yours."

Allison stared at him for a few seconds before smirking. "I was expecting more from you, Clint Adams."

"Why?"

"Because there's an animal out there killing innocent girls. Doesn't that bother you?"

Slowly, deliberately, Clint set down the strip of bacon he'd been working on and then picked up his napkin. He wiped off his mouth, and when he placed the napkin down, he did so with just enough force to rattle the cups and plates in front of them. "Who are you after?"

"The man who—"

"No," Clint interrupted. "I asked who, not what. Tell me a name. Give me a description, give me anything that makes this killer something more than a monster from a bad dream."

Allison's features hardened with raw defiance. Her eyes became like icy steel balls set in their sockets. "I don't have to tell you anything."

"No? But you were more than willing to sit here and have this little chat with me and all but ask me to come on the path with you so you can have some extra firepower once you get wherever the hell it is you're going."

"Is that what you think I am? Just some gunhand? If that's the case, you made an awfully big mistake, lady. And if you think you're doing any good by wasting your life tearing after a ghost, than you might as well find a spot next to your sister's grave and stay there because there's not much difference between you and her right now.

"Actually," Clint added when he saw that Allison was just about to explode, "there is a difference. Your sister doesn't have a choice in where she is right now. You do. In fact, so do I, and I don't feel like blazing from one town to another looking at dead girls without anything else to go on."

Clint sat in his chair and kept his eyes fixed upon Allison for a few seconds after he'd said his piece. He knew he'd lit a fire under her, which had been his intention. He'd played more than enough poker to know when he was being shown someone's game face. Although he knew that she was being forthright about her sister, he also knew that she thought she was controlling him like a puppet on a string.

That simply would not do.

After another few heartbeats, Clint was still sitting on the edge of his seat and Allison was still staring straight back at him. Both of them had put up rock walls, and it was obvious that she wasn't about to take hers down.

"All right," Clint said as he got up and tossed some money onto the table. "That's settled. Enjoy your vendetta, but leave Jeremiah out of it."

Without another word, Clint put his hat on and walked for the front door. He made it all the way outside before he heard anyone coming after him. And even when he did hear the footsteps hurrying to catch up, he didn't stop walking until he was outside and across the street.

"Adams," came Allison's voice. There was a stern, demanding tone in it that obviously ruffled Clint's feathers even more. Finally, she stopped and spoke again. "Clint! Wait." Letting out a weary breath, she added, "Please."

Clint stopped and turned around. Rather than make her walk up to him, she went to her. "Now that sounds better."

"You're right," she said. "I've been doing this for a while and I guess I might have picked up some bad habits along the way. But with the men I've had to deal with, I haven't had much choice."

He nodded. "I understand."

"But you were wrong about something else."

"Just one thing?" Clint asked with a smirk. "That would be a switch."

As she allowed herself to laugh at his joke, she lost a bit more of the steely edge that had showed itself inside the restaurant. That didn't last too long, however, and her voice soon took on a more serious tone. "The killer I'm after isn't a ghost."

"You know something about him?"

Allison nodded. "I've had a word with some who might know something about him."

"Would you be willing to tell me what you've found out?"

Again, she nodded. "But only if you agree to help me track him down."

"That's going to have to wait."

"Wait? Why?"

"Because it looks like we've got some bigger concerns right about now."

SIXTEEN

Allison noticed that Clint was looking at something over her shoulder. When she turned to get a look for herself, she had no trouble at all spotting the group of dirty-faced men approaching them.

"I count three of them," Clint said in a whisper that only reached Allison's ears. When the men fanned out a bit more, he added, "Make that four. Are these friends of yours?"

Shaking her head, Allison said, "Nope. I was just about to ask you the same question."

"Could they be friends of someone else you might have talked to before coming here?"

Hearing that, Allison cringed a little as she glanced over at Clint. "That's a possibility."

"Great," Clint said as he squared his shoulders. "This is just great." He put on a smile and faced the four men. "How are you boys doing this morning?"

One of the men stepped up from the other three. They were all big fellows wearing clothes that looked as though they'd been slept in for at least an entire week. There was just as much dirt on their faces as there was on their boots, and the teeth they showed when they glared at Clint didn't look much better.

"You'd be Clint Adams?" the first man asked.

"That's the rumor."

"Then you're the man we're after."

Clint looked over to Allison and got nothing more than a confused shrug for his trouble. Looking back to the four men, he asked, "What can I do for you?"

"You can start by telling me why you've been spreading so much shit around town behind our backs."

"Pardon me?"

"You heard what I said."

"Yeah," grunted one of the other three men. "And we heard what you said."

"Shut the fuck up, Pete," the first one snarled. "We was more'n willin' to let you strut around here like you owned the place, Adams. But we ain't about to stand for nobody talking about us behind our backs."

"Look," Clint said, doing his level best to keep his tone even and not show the aggravation that was building up inside of him. "I don't know who any of you are and I've got no reason to talk about any of you behind your backs."

"We saw what you done in Kylie's," the first one said. "That don't mean none of us are afraid of you."

"I've still got to see the judge about that," Clint pointed out. "Now, why would I want to start anything else? I don't even have my gun." As he said that, Clint pulled open the flap of his jacket to show the empty spot around his waist where his holster should have been. What they didn't know was that the New Line was tucked in his belt at the small of his back.

The four men must have been even more tightly wound than Clint had guessed, because that movement was enough to put a spark to the already short fuse.

All four men reacted at the same time. They went for their guns and started unleashing a torrent of curses that was all but gibberish once the gunshots started roaring through the air.

The moment Clint saw what was about to happen, he reacted. While his reflexes were as sharp as ever, he was still slowed by the fact that he had to waste a fraction of a second to keep himself from trying to draw his Colt. Since the modified pistol was still in the sheriff's custody, it wasn't about to do him much good now. And another shooting incident wouldn't bode well for him, either.

Hoping that his split-second delay wouldn't cost him too dearly, Clint launched himself toward Allison with both arms outstretched. "Down!" he shouted.

She was already twisting at the waist when he got to her. Even so, Allison managed to brace herself for Clint's impact and roll with it once he knocked her off her feet.

As they dropped to the boardwalk, Clint on top of Allison, shots roared in their ears and bullets hissed in the air over their heads. They slammed against the boards, and Clint pressed himself down on top of her until the first volley of gunshots had passed.

Oddly enough, Allison looked more relaxed and her smile was more genuine now than ever before. Clint could feel her heart slamming against his chest and could feel the heat from her excited breaths as they lingered together for those moments.

Allison's legs closed around him just a bit. It wasn't more than a second, but the feel of it went through both of them like an entire summer's day.

"Excuse me," she whispered. "But I think it's my turn."

Before Clint could respond, he felt Allison push him up a bit so she could roll out from under him. As she moved, she pulled her weapon from its holster, and had brought it up by the time she was laying on her stomach facing the other four men.

Gritting her teeth, she squeezed off a few rounds. Although she didn't have the time or the angle to aim properly, her shots were enough to scatter the four men before they could unleash another storm of lead.

The boardwalk pounded against Allison's body where she was laying flat against it. One quick glance over her shoulder was all she needed to tell her that she didn't have to shift her aim toward the heavy steps. Those steps belonged to Clint, and there were only two more of them before he'd reached the edge of the boardwalk.

Having practically jumped over Allison's prone body, Clint kept his head down low as he rushed forward. He pushed off the crooked edge of the boardwalk with one foot while stretching his other leg out to catch him. The moment his boot touched the ground, he planted it and pushed to one side.

It wasn't the most graceful maneuver, but it was just enough to get him closer to the gunmen while avoiding the few scattered shots that came his way as he moved. Of course, now that he had to contend with the gunmen at point-blank range, Clint was hoping he hadn't bitten off more than he could chew.

SEVENTEEN

Killing all those sweet little girls had been such a delight. Every last one of them had brought such distinct joy to the man who'd taken their lives. Each one of them had shown him a new flavor of pleasure that he would never taste again.

As he stood at the side of the street watching Clint Adams and Allison Little fight for their lives, the killer felt yet another kind of joy that sent a ripple under his skin. He was practiced at keeping his emotions from showing, just as he was practiced at keeping himself from being noticed at critical times.

The spot he'd chosen to view this show had been picked just as carefully as the words he'd used to start the fight in the first place. Of course, neither of those tasks had been too difficult.

Those brutes were as stupid as sheep and just as willing to be led by anyone who pointed them in a direction. A few harsh words tossed in the wrong direction were certain to ruffle some feathers. All the killer had needed to do was make the words a little harsher, toss them with a little more force and make sure they landed. After that, it was all too easy to drop Clint's name and send those gun-toting idiots along their way.

Watching the ruckus he'd started, the killer shifted his eyes toward Allison. She was every bit as pretty as her sister had been, despite the fact that she'd grown too old for his tastes. Even so, she might be worthy of an exception. The more he watched her, the more the killer wanted to feel her skin on his hands, her blood on his fingers.

And then there was Adams.

Adams was like a storm in a bottle. The way he held himself back from simply cutting through every last one of those assholes was impressive. Still, the killer felt himself growing frustrated, even though he was fairly certain that Adams would hold himself back until it was absolutely necessary to do more.

The killer had heard of Adams here and there, but that didn't mean much to him. All he relied upon was his instincts. They were sharper than the blades he carried and had been honed through years of being chased by all matter of man.

And they called *him* a savage.

That word rolled through the killer's mind as he watched the fight flare up like a fire that had been doused with kerosene.

They called him a savage when they found the girls that were left behind. They didn't know the joy those girls had caused. They didn't even appreciate the trouble the killer had gone through to make sure they made it back to their families every bit as pretty as when they'd been taken.

Prettier, even.

The killer was called a savage for doing what only came natural to him. They hunted him just as men before them had hunted everyone he'd known. Just as he now hunted the sweet, pretty girls who were his only source of joy.

"Well," he thought with a smirk. "Not the only source."

He also had Clint Adams and Allison Little to keep him amused.

The determination on Allison's face was intoxicating.

The confusion on Adams's was priceless.

By the look of things, however, the killer's amusement might not last for much longer.

EIGHTEEN

Allison inched forward so she could get a cleaner shot. She couldn't help but feel the excitement rush through her like a wave as she watched Clint move. She'd heard plenty about him, but seeing him in action was something altogether different.

Even though the shots coming from the other men were getting closer by the second, she found herself stretching her neck out so she could get a better look at Clint. He was the most unpredictable man she'd ever seen. Even so, the look on his face showed that he knew exactly what he was doing.

One shot hissed through the air, slicing a path that brushed through Allison's hair and clipped her just enough to push her head down without doing much damage. She felt the ground rock beneath her as she reached up to feel the spot where the bullet had passed. Although there was some blood on her hand, there wasn't enough to worry about.

"You all right back there?" Clint asked.

Even though he had plenty to keep him busy, Clint still managed to notice when Allison had been grazed. It was at that moment she gave Clint more admiration than any man she'd met in the last half of her life.

"I'm fine," she replied quickly while squeezing off a shot toward the group of rowdies. "Just worry about yourself!"

Clint heard the desperation in Allison's voice and ducked while turning back around. The move came more out of reflex and experience than anything else. Sure enough, one of the men who'd started this whole thing had been trying to take advantage of the moment when Clint's back had been turned.

A beefy fist rushed toward the back of his head. Once Clint had moved, however, that fist knocked against the top of his head instead. The impact was jarring, but nothing too serious.

Before the other man had a chance to realize his punch had missed, Clint's elbow was paying him back for taking the swing in the first place. That elbow slammed into the man's midsection, doubling him over while driving out all the wind from his lungs in the process.

The man crumpled and staggered half a step, putting him in perfect position for Clint to finish him off. All it took was a quick, ferocious lift of his knee and the man's head was snapping back to leave a spray of blood in the air.

The fellow went over like a sack of dirt, almost knocking one of his friends over as well.

"Son of a bitch!" one of the others grunted when he saw his friend fall over. He, like the others by now, had a gun in his hand and was more than willing to use it. His eyes were almost glazed over as he snapped his pistol to aim at Clint.

After tossing himself into the mix, Clint had actually given himself some time to think while throwing the others off their balance. It really wasn't more than a second or two, but it was all he needed. In that short stretch of time, Clint had picked his next several options. When he saw that gun coming his way, those options were whittled down to one.

Clint reached out with an open hand and immediately

felt the other man's wrist slap against his palm. After clenching his fingers around that wrist, Clint twisted hard until the man let out a pained yelp. Bones grated together and started to crack, until the man's fingers loosened and his gun popped out from his grasp.

With his free hand, Clint caught the gun as best he could. Unfortunately, he was only able to grab it around the middle instead of by the handle. That was good enough for him to return the gun to its owner in a quick jab to the fellow's jaw.

Iron crunched against bone once and then once again before the only thing holding the man upright was Clint's grip around his wrist. Once that was relaxed, the man fell back and dropped to the ground, where he lay sprawled on top of his fallen partner.

Shots were still blasting through the air, but not one of them seemed to be coming from the same direction twice. And though Clint could hear the lead hissing all around him, that too was wild. A quick pat-down and look at himself told him that he hadn't been hit just yet. That would surely change, however, if the fight lasted too much longer.

Twisting around while getting the pistol in his hand properly, Clint got a quick look at his surroundings. He was still in the thick of things, although the participants were dwindling down to a manageable number.

Two men were left. One of those looked to be about ready to cut and run since fire from Allison's gun was keeping him hopping from one spot to another. That left only one other, who also happened to be the one that had been trying to take a shot at Clint.

The man aiming at Clint now was the one someone else had called Pete. Smoke curled from Pete's gun and he swallowed hard to try and steady the pounding of his heart.

"This is a misunderstanding, Pete," Clint said. "Whatever you heard, I didn't say anything about anyone behind their back. I don't even know who you fellows are."

Pete's eyes darted back and forth. When he got a look at his friend, he was just in time to see that man fire off another round before taking a bullet in the shoulder.

The impact knocked the third man violently off his feet as blood spewed from the freshly opened wound. When he hit the ground on his back, the man let out a grunt. From there, he started squirming around and cussing under his breath like a pissed off turtle that had been flipped onto his back.

Clint had already lowered his gun and was about to give Pete the chance to do the same. After seeing his friend catch a bullet, Pete was in no mood to talk. That was just enough to push him over the edge, and when he reeled back toward Clint, all reason had left his eyes.

Clint dropped to one knee while bringing up the pistol he'd taken. When his knee touched the ground, the final rattle of shots went off like the final salvo of a fireworks show.

Pete pulled his trigger while his friend with the shoulder wound did the same.

Allison fired a round at the fallen man to stop him before he got a chance to aim, assuming Clint would be able to take down Pete with time to spare.

The pistol in Clint's hand barked once and sent its round through the air. The bullet drilled a hole through Pete's skull, snapping his head back and emptying it in a pulpy mist.

For a moment, Pete seemed to have found a second wind. He lifted his head and stared out at Clint. That lasted for a full second before his knees buckled and his eyes rolled up into their sockets. Letting out his final breath, Pete fell over and landed in a heap.

"Dammit," Clint snarled as he tossed the gun from his hand.

Ignoring the fact that the man was still holding a gun, Clint walked over to the last of the attackers who was still conscious and reached down to take hold of him by the collar. Planting one foot on the man's gun hand, Clint rested all of his weight down on it as he leaned in to glare directly into the fellow's eyes.

"Tell me what brought this on," Clint demanded. "I want to know what you heard, where you heard it and who told it to you."

At first the man started to turn his head away, but was pulled back to face Clint by a vicious tug from his collar.

"I've had enough of you already," Clint snarled. "Start talking!"

NINETEEN

Although they'd fled once things seemed to be getting messy, the people on the street were closing in now that the fight was over. Most of them weren't willing to step in directly just yet, but there were still things to do and places to be.

Clint didn't pay any of those others any mind. None of them were close enough to catch his attention, and it wouldn't be long before the other three attackers would come to their senses.

When he didn't get anything from the last of the gunmen, Clint cocked his head in warning and started slowly grinding his heel against the ground. Since his wrist was still pinned beneath that heel, the man on the ground started to squirm.

"Come on," Clint said. "I'm waiting."

Coming up behind him, Allison patted Clint once on the back to let him know she was there. "If he doesn't want to talk, then to hell with him," she said offhandedly. "We're within our rights killing him, so let's be done with it."

She waited a little over a second before cocking back the hammer of her pistol and pointing it at the man's face. That brought his eyes up to her real quickly. When he got a

76

look at the casual indifference in Allison's features, his mouth opened and words started spilling out.

"Wait, wait!" the man squealed. "I'll tell you anything! Just don't shoot!"

"What brought all this on?" Clint asked.

"It's like they said. Pete heard something about you spouting off behind his back."

"Why would I do that?"

"I don't know. Since you got to town everyone's been talking about you. That is, once they found out who you are. Pete was thinking he'd like to call you out, but it was all just talk. I swear!"

"All talk?" Clint asked. "Until now, you mean?"

The man did his best to nod, but found it difficult since he was being pressed against the ground and was wriggling uncomfortably to boot.

"What was he supposed to have said?" Allison asked.

The man couldn't take his eyes off Clint. He gaped up at him as though he was staring into the face of Death itself. "I don't even know. All I know is that once he heard it, Pete and Cory got their tails in a knot and said they had to shut your mouth before folks around here started thinking they were yellow. They got whoever they could find and came here."

"How'd they know where to find me?" Clint asked.

"I guess they heard it from somewhere."

Allison looked over to Clint and added, "Or was told by whoever lit the match to this whole thing."

"Maybe," the man said as if trying to latch onto any explanation he could to appease Clint. "They dragged us along and took us here, saying you would be here. They knew you'd be here."

Clint was feeling his guts twist up more now than when the lead had been flying. As much as he wanted to wring more out of the man under his boot, he simply knew there wasn't much more to be had. As it was, the man was grasping at straws just to stay alive.

By the look on her face, it seemed that Allison was thinking along those same lines. She let out a breath, shrugged and lifted her gun one more time. "All right then," she said with a sigh. "Since you proved to be as useful as tits on a bull, then there's no reason to keep you around."

With that and nothing more, she sighted down the barrel of her pistol and prepared to pull her trigger.

"Wait! Wait!" the man hollered.

"Not this again," Allison groaned.

"I might have seen the man who talked to Pete."

Allison shook her head. "Now you're just blowing smoke."

"No! Honest. It wasn't much, but I think I saw Pete turn back and talk to someone who—"

The man's head snapped to one side as if it had been twisted by a set of vicious, invisible hands. Blood sprayed from his skull as the sound of a rifle shot cracked through the air. Between the noises of the town all around him and the ringing in his own ears from the gunfire, Clint wasn't able to hear the shot until the bullet had already found its mark.

Clint looked up to see if he could find any trace of the gun that had just killed the man on the ground in front of him. All he could see was a whole bunch of confused people scattering on the street after hearing the same, fatal shot.

Allison was looking around as well, searching for any trace of the shooter. "I think it came from over there," she said, pointing toward the other side of the street.

Clint looked in that direction, which wasn't much of a help. Besides the fact that he'd already figured on his own that the shot had to have come from that direction, there was far too much going on to pick anything out in particular.

There were people standing and staring in disbelief at the bloody scene. There were just as many people turning their backs or even trying to get away without breaking into a run.

Horses were walking and carts were being pulled.

Faces stared out from nearly every window.

By the time he'd taken all of this in, Clint knew only too well that if the shooter had wanted to get away, he would have been able to get to the other side of town by now.

Both Clint and Allison shifted their eyes to the man at their feet.

"Is he . . . ?" she asked hopefully.

Clint let out his breath and stood up from where he'd been kneeling at the other man's side. Shaking his head, he replied, "He's gone. And so is whoever did this, I'd imagine."

"You think whoever shot him was aiming for you?"

After thinking about that for a moment, Clint shook his head again. "It's possible, but I doubt it. More than likely, it was whoever got this fight going in the first place."

"And he's probably the one we've been after anyway. At least we know he's still close by."

"Yeah," Clint said under his breath. "And if it were quieter around here, I bet we could hear him laughing right now."

TWENTY

The killer's face was a mask. It reflected nothing of what he'd just done or what was going through his mind. In fact, as he turned and walked down the alley with the smoking rifle in his hand, the expression on his face was downright pleasant.

To anyone who came up to him right then and there, he looked as if he was out for a stroll and was taking a short-cut to the next street.

Not that anyone would bother to look, however. Everyone around him was too busy gaping at the spectacle across the street or trying their best to get away from it. A few faces had turned at the sound of the shot he'd taken, but were distracted soon after by the bloody results.

Strolling down the narrow corridor between buildings, the killer picked an inviting stack of old crates and set the rifle down behind them. It might be found and it might not. Either way, he knew the show would go on.

Pretty Allison would keep chasing after him with that wonderful fire in her eyes. If only she knew how close she'd come over the last few months. Part of the killer wanted to tell her that she'd even laid eyes on him once or twice, just so he could see the anger on her face.

And then there was Clint Adams. That one had been real close as well, but not to the same thing as Allison.

Only a minute or two ago, the killer had had Adams in his sights. No matter what was going on around him, the killer's hand remained steady and his aim remained fixed. All it would have taken was a pull of a trigger and Adams would have been dead.

Or maybe not.

Thinking back to it, the killer swore that Adams had twitched at the right moment or moved at another critical time, as though he could feel the rifle lining up to him. Taking a shot at a man like Adams was like getting one shot at a grizzly.

It had better be a killing shot, because anything else would mean certain death for whoever had botched the job.

That broke the pleasantness of the killer's face.

It made him smile.

No, Adams was way too entertaining to kill just yet. Men like Adams were a big reason why the killer savored every second of what he did. It was men like Adams who thought they were above the law and took it upon themselves to spill all the blood their hearts desired just because they had the power to do so.

Men like Adams looked down their noses at certain people just because they thought they were better than them. And if Adams was better than certain people, that gave him the right to force his will upon them and take away everything those other people had.

Men like Adams were all over the place. They were in the Army; they wore badges; they even pounded their gavels in courts of law.

With that thought; the killer's smile got even wider.

Clint's trial was coming up before too long. Now, with this recent scuffle to add to the list of charges, the spectacle would be even more entertaining. That was yet another reason for Clint's life to be spared. Watching someone like the high and mighty Gunsmith hang would be almost too much entertainment to bear.

Nodding to himself, the killer knew he'd made the right decision in killing that asshole before he babbled too much, rather than shooting Adams himself. At least Adams was funny to watch as he ran in circles like a coyote chasing its tail. But that other one looked like he was talking too much.

That simply would not do.

As much as the killer enjoyed a good challenge, there was no reason to let the advantage tip too far away from him.

Emerging from the alley, the killer averted his eyes and put on yet another mask. This time, he allowed himself to look the part that everyone thought he should play when they first got a look at him. As long as he didn't go against the grain too much, the killer found that he could pretty much go where he pleased without drawing any attention.

Besides, after hearing all the gunshots, folks had plenty more to fret about than him.

Adams would die soon enough. When it happened, it would certainly be something better than just a bullet to the head. His death would be slow and such a sight to behold that it would stick in the killer's mind forever.

And then it would be Allison's turn.

Pretty, pretty Allison.

TWENTY-ONE

Clint knew the law would be coming for him. The only thing that surprised him was the fact that they weren't there already.

Once the smoke had cleared, two men were dead and another two just about wished they were. The surviving pair of attackers opened their eyes and winced with pain, finding themselves on their backs at the side of the street.

For a moment, both of those men looked as if they would break out laughing. Then they caught sight of the bodies of the other two and their smirks were gone. When they got a look at Clint standing nearby, they looked like they wanted to start running.

"Easy, now, easy," said the doctor who'd arrived moments ago. "How are you feeling?"

"I'm fine," the man said as he tried to jump to his feet. After getting knocked out, that wasn't the smartest of moves. As soon as he was upright, he wobbled and almost fell over again if the doctor hadn't been there to steady him.

"Get that bastard away from me," the second man said. "He damn near killed me. Look what he done to Pete!"

Although most of the crowd had drifted away, there were still a few who wanted to watch until the show was truly over. A few of those picked this as their moment to join in.

"You four picked the fight," one of the crowd said. "We saw it."

"Yeah! Where's the sheriff?"

As more and more of the bystanders started lending their own voices to the mix, the two surviving gunmen shut their mouths.

"I'd like to have a word with you two," Clint said as he stepped forward.

Allison was right by his side, her hand resting on her holstered pistol. "That makes two of us."

The first wounded man reached for the spot on his belt where his own gun was normally tucked. When his palm slapped against nothing but leather and his own gut, he held out both hands to ward Clint off. "You're right, mister. This was all a mistake. Whatever you said, it don't matter no more. Right?"

Clint shook his head and kept walking forward.

Suddenly, moments before Clint was close enough to reach out and take hold of the other man, someone else was between them.

"That'll be enough of that," came a bellowing voice.

The man who'd put himself between Clint and the other man was short and chubby with long, wild hair. Although he'd been sure enough of himself at first, some of that confidence went out the window once Clint shifted his eyes to look directly at him.

At first, Clint was going to move the other man out of his way. He stopped himself short, however, when he spotted the badge pinned to his chest. "Stand aside, Deputy," Clint said. "I've still got business with these two."

Dell's chest was heaving, and he struggled to keep his labored breaths from sounding too loud. He lost that battle real quickly, however, and let out a gasp after a gulping wheeze. "There won't be . . . any of that. Not until . . . I hear what the hell happened here."

"Maybe you should ask them," Allison said as she stabbed a finger toward the two men being tended by the doctor. "They're the ones who started it."

Glancing around to everyone around him and then looking down at the bodies sprawled upon the ground, Dell looked absolutely flustered. The more he looked at it all, the more out of his element he seemed.

"Look here, now," Dell said. "Sheriff Hayes is on the trail of a killer, and I won't have any more trouble while he's gone."

"They started it!" someone from the crowd shouted. "That man and lady were in the restaurant and those four jumped them. That man weren't even armed!"

More and more voices joined in with that same sentiment. Some of them even started calling the attackers by name just so they could curse them personally. Soon, Clint realized that all he needed to do was stand back and let things run their course.

"Enough of that!" Dell shouted. "You two are coming with me," he said to the wounded gunmen. Nodding toward Clint and Allison, he added, "You two aren't out of this yet."

A slender man wearing a brown suit rushed from the same direction that the deputy had come from. Although he was in a hurry to get to the deputy's side, he stopped short when he got a better look at what was going on.

"Dell, where have you been?" the slender man said. "Didn't you call for me to meet you outside of town?"

"I sure did, Ernie," Dell replied. "But something came up."

"Um yes, I can see that."

"You wanted to help me?"

"Of course. That's why I—"

"Then pick up one of them guns by your feet and help me bring these fellas in."

The slender man looked down at the ground and found that a pistol wasn't too far away. When he spotted the weapon, he jumped as though the gun was a snake poised to bite him.

Dell kicked the gun a little closer to him. "Don't worry. You won't be getting much trouble from these two. Looks like all the real trouble's over."

"You want us to lend a hand?" Clint asked.

"You two have done enough. You, especially. The only reason you won't be coming to jail with me is because I'm a little shorthanded right now."

"If that's what you want, then we'll go peacefully." Clint spotted Allison starting to protest, but stopped her with a quick, gentle nudge. "Both of us," he said before she got a chance to open her mouth.

Looking at each of them carefully, Dell slowly started to shake his head. "I may not know you two very well, but I've known most of these other folks most of my life. If they all say you're not to blame, there must be something to it. Besides, guilty people tend to run off when they see the law coming."

Clint helped get the other wounded man to his feet and shoved him forward as the deputy started walking. "Not to mention the fact that you've still got my gun."

"You could've gotten another gun at three different stores here in town. Still, this won't look too good when you stand in front of Judge Zellner tomorrow."

The other men were coming along quietly. In fact, they had their heads down and their arms limp as though there was nothing else for them to do besides shuffle along to keep from getting hurt. In fact, Ernie Niedelander walked behind them all in much the same way.

"His hearing is tomorrow?" Allison asked.

Dell nodded. "I'm sure once the sheriff hears about this, he'll want to get it over with as soon as possible."

"We're probably both official troublemakers by now," Clint said to Allison. "Am I right, Deputy?"

"For the moment."

"Will you speak up for us at trial?"

"Sheriff Hayes is the one you should be more concerned about. He'll be the one dealing with you when it's all said and done."

Allison let out a short, humorless laugh. "The one to hang us, you mean."

"Maybe," Dell said. "Or he might just want to deputize you."

TWENTY-TWO

This time, when the smoke had cleared and the law was done with him, Clint wasn't the only one walking away without a gun at his side. Allison's weapon had been taken by the deputy as well, and she acted as though she was suddenly missing one of her feet. Her steps were more than a little uncertain and the frustration on her face was easy enough to see. Clint was just glad the deputy hadn't searched him and found the New Line.

"How long have you been after this killer?" Clint asked.

Allison pulled in a breath. "Feels like forever."

"I can tell."

Hearing that was like a splash of cold water in her face. She blinked quickly a few times and put on a smile. "Just because we got caught this once doesn't mean we're through."

"Not hardly."

"I like the sound of that, Clint Adams." Stepping closer, she reached out to slip her arms around his waist. "And I like the way you handled yourself back there. I feel like you would have gone to the end to protect me. Thanks for that."

Resting one hand on her hip, Clint placed his other hand

under her chin and felt the smooth skin leading down to her neck. "In case you weren't watching, those men were after me. Maybe I should be the one to thank you."

"I would've gotten to them sooner or later," she replied.

They looked into each other's eyes for a moment, each of them carefully studying the other. Before too much time had passed, Clint became aware of the eyes that were being focused on them from practically every other direction.

"Looks like we're drawing another crowd," he said.

Allison looked around casually. After being disarmed and dismissed by the sheriff's deputy, they'd walked down the street a ways from where they'd been attacked. Although the commotion was over and folks were wandering back to wherever they needed to be, word and rumor were spreading about the excitement that had happened a few minutes ago.

When she caught one of the locals staring directly at her, Allison would return the stare with one of her own. That local would quickly snap his or her eyes away and shuffle off as if caught peeping into a window.

"Let them look," she said. "At least we gave them something else to talk about besides that poor girl that was killed."

"Speaking of which, you might not want to go chasing everyone off just yet."

"Why not?"

Clint looked down at her as if he couldn't believe why she would have asked that question. Allison stared right back with a mix of playful seduction and the same spark she'd shown to the intruding locals.

"I'll tell you why not," Clint replied. "Because one of these people might have seen who took that last shot."

Shrugging, Allison looked over toward that part of the street. "All I need to know is that he's still in town."

"And how can you be so sure of that?"

"Because he's not the type to run so easily. I've been after him long enough to know that much about him." Her eyes shifted around, as if to take in every surrounding doorway, rooftop and window. "He's still here. If I close my eyes, I can feel him watching." When she looked back to Clint, she added, "That's probably why I don't close my eyes too much."

"Actually, that might work to our advantage."

"How?"

"Because that way we won't miss anything that we happen to find while we're looking across the street from our little scuffle. I know the shot came from that general direction at least, so that gives us a place to start."

"I've been tracking this bastard for a while now and I've never found someone like you."

Clint had already started to walk toward the first spot he wanted to check when he heard her say that. Those words caused him to stop in his tracks, turn around and ask, "Someone like me?"

Nodding, Allison stepped up beside him and kept pace as they walked toward the other side of the street. "Someone who doesn't go with the rest of the pack no matter what points him in that direction."

"You mean with the sheriff."

"That's right."

"So you don't think he's on the right track?"

She shook her head. "Nope," she said matter-of-factly.

"How do you know?"

"Because I've seen it before."

"And you just let everyone go off without trying to steer them in another direction? I'm sure Hayes or someone might be open to suggestion."

A smirk broke across her face, and it seemed that Allison might just start to laugh. "You know better that that, Clint. You've got to."

"Haven't you ever tried?"

"Talking to the law? Sure. I tried that at first. And they

were real willing to listen to me, pat me on my head and send me along my way. I've gotten close to that killer a few times and you know what? I think that was because the killer let me get close just to watch me squirm."

Listening to the tone in her voice, Clint could tell that Allison wasn't just guessing about what she said. There was something about her manner and way of speaking that told him she was holding a real hand rather than some cocky bluff.

"It happens a lot," she continued. "It might take the law a while, but they always take off after their wild Indian, disappear for a bit and come back. Sometimes they even come back with a body, holding it up like they're so damn proud."

"You mean they always go after an Indian?"

She nodded.

"And sometimes they find one?"

She nodded again, only more solemnly this time.

"That sounds like a real nice setup for a killer," Clint said. "He gets to do what he wants, lay down a false trail and let the law run down it. If he makes sure the trail leads somewhere, then he gets to move on free and clear to some other place to start all over again."

Suddenly, Clint felt Allison's arms wrap around him as she pressed her lips against his in a fierce, passionate kiss.

"What was that for?" Clint asked with surprise.

"For being the first clearheaded man I've run into in a long while."

TWENTY-THREE

After all the riding he'd done and all the ground he'd covered, it took something special to catch Clint by surprise anymore. Every now and then, however, he was surprised by something that was relatively simple. Some might say it was even a bit of common sense. Even so, Clint could not get over how so many people could be so oblivious to what was going on around them.

After he and Allison split up to try and talk to the familiar faces that were still around after the gunfight, Clint soon felt his frustration reaching a new height. With respect and a smile on his face, he approached folks doing nothing but standing and talking to their neighbors. He approached shop owners who'd come out to witness the spectacle for themselves. He even approached folks who'd been sitting on the boardwalk with their feet dangling onto the street during the fight and were still sitting in that same position.

Every last one of those folks had plenty to say.

Unfortunately, it was a whole lot of nothing.

Half of the folks Clint spoke to were too concerned patting him on the back or admiring his style to be of much help. The other half were too afraid of him to say anything but what they thought he wanted to hear. When he looked over to check on Allison's progress, he could tell that she wasn't getting much more than he was.

A little while later, they met up in a spot roughly half a block away from where the fight had been in the first place.

"Did you find out anything?" Clint asked without getting his hopes up.

"Sure I did," Allison replied. "That we're practically heroes for taking down those loudmouthed assholes before they hurt anyone else. You know we can get free drinks in half the saloons in town for taking care of them the way we did."

"Anything else?"

"You mean anything useful?" Allison paused and then shook her head. "Not really. How about you?"

"Pretty much the same. Although some of the folks tended to look back this way when I asked them about that last rifle shot."

"Me, too," Allison said. "They didn't really know about where it came from. Some even said they didn't remember hearing a last shot, but they mostly looked over in this direction."

Both of them found themselves looking in the same general area as the people had when they'd talked to them. Clint and Allison were mulling over what they'd heard while looking at the spot in question one more time.

Suddenly, Clint felt a burst of excitement. "Hold it," he said. "Don't move." ·

Allison froze like a startled deer. Her eyes snapped over to Clint, making her seem like an anxious little girl playing statue. "Why?"

"Look at us," Clint said.

She did. Every time her eyes went back and forth between Clint and the area around them, Allison became increasingly frustrated. "Am I supposed to be seeing something? Because if I am, I'm just not seeing it."

"I think we both heard or saw something that was more useful than we thought," Clint pointed out. "I didn't even realize it until just now."

"Could you tell me what it is? My neck's getting stiff."

"We both talked to some people and watched them look in the same direction."

Allison didn't seem to be satisfied by Clint's explanation, or even to understand why he was getting so worked up. Then, after thinking about it for another moment, she saw the same thing that Clint had spotted.

"That alley," she said, breaking suddenly out of her frozen stance. "They all looked back to that alley."

Clint was nodding. "So did the people I spoke to. They were all just glances, and they were all looking back this way. And I don't think anyone was looking up."

"Me neither. I would've noticed that."

"All right then," Clint said decisively. "I guess we know where we've got to look next."

TWENTY-FOUR

The trail was going cold. Hayes could tell that much after only a few minutes of trying to follow it.

First of all, even if the tracks he'd found had belonged to the killer, they were at least a day or two old. That much was plain enough for anyone to see. Secondly, those same tracks only led about a hundred yards in one direction before they become so faint that they could have gone anywhere after that.

The sheriff reined in his horse and motioned for all of his men to do the same. Although they were anxious to keep moving, the deputies pulled back on their own reins until they were able to form a semicircle around their leader.

"You find anything else out there, Mason?" Hayes asked the man who'd taken the longest to form up around him.

Mason wore a scowl on his face that was even deeper than usual. He was a talented hunter and had some genuine tracking skill. Like most hunters, however, he was much more comfortable alone in the wild than in any group.

"I found some things," Mason said.

"I'm not just looking for things," the sheriff replied sternly. "I'm looking for something that will bring us closer to the animal that's hiding out there. You find any-thing that could point us in that one's direction?"

Mason took a moment to think that over. He was never quick to answer at any time, but this one stuck in his craw a little longer. Finally, he gave half a shrug. "Could be."

"Then why don't you take one other and see what you can find."

"Who should I take?"

"That's up to you. Just pick now because you two might be camping for a while."

The rest of the men knew those words were directed as much to them as they were to Mason. A few of the deputies had their own thoughts about the hunter, and most of those thoughts weren't too good. If they wanted to go along with him, they could make that known. If not, they could make that known as well.

Looking around at the deputies' faces, Mason saw some who looked away and some who met his eyes with strength. He nodded toward one of the latter and said, "What about Chapman?"

Sheriff Hayes nodded. "That'd be my choice, too."

"You sure, Sheriff?" Chapman asked. "We might be gone for a while, like you said."

"I need to head back into town. As much as I'd like to think otherwise, I doubt that everyone there's going to be-have themselves while we're gone. Folks know the both of you are good at what you do, though. They'll take comfort in knowing you boys are still out here on the trail."

Mason's face twisted as if he'd just gotten a taste of something sour. "You sayin' this is all for show?"

"Not hardly. I expect to find this animal. I just don't want him to double back and have free rein over an un-guarded henhouse."

The hunter smirked and nodded. He then tugged at his reins and pointed his horse in the direction the tracks were headed.

"We'll signal when we find something worth telling you about," Chapman said.

Hayes acknowledged that and added, "Be sure to report back in three days, no matter what. We can regroup from there and decide where to go next."

Whether or not the rest of the men understood what was really being said didn't matter. All that did matter was that Chapman knew what was going through the sheriff's mind.

Three days.

After that, the search would either be abandoned or over. Life had to move on, killers or not. There would always be wolves prowling in the dark places. It was just better for the sheep if that wasn't such a widely known fact.

"What about the rest of us?" one of the younger deputies asked. "We can help. I done plenty of hunting."

"Yeah," one of the others offered. "And my pa's done his share of tracking. He taught me everything he knows."

"Your pa can barely walk when the weather's too cold," Hayes said. "And this isn't some deer hunt. Chapman and Mason are the best men for this job. Any of you who think differently can step up and tell them why they should step down."

Hayes looked around at the faces of his deputies. Although he didn't want a confrontation, he half expected one anyway. It was a pleasant surprise when nobody took the bait he'd offered.

"All right then," Hayes said. "That's settled."

Seeing that his message was clear, Hayes tipped his hat in a curt farewell before turning his horse back toward town. A quick look around at the rest of his men told him that either they hadn't picked up on his message to Chapman or had enough sense to take it for what it was.

Although his deputies were well intentioned, Hayes knew that some of them were a bit too young to take on all parts of the job. Most of them signed on to do the right thing or even to see some action that was sanctioned by the badge they wore. That didn't mean that all of them were ready to accept some of the dirtier aspects of the role.

There was a time to chase down the bad men and a time to let them go. That was never easy for the younger fellas to handle. All too often, Hayes had bumped heads with a wide-eyed youngster about the difference between turning your back on a problem and putting things into their proper perspective.

By the looks of it, the sheriff had gotten his point across to the right people. The younger ones would be getting back to town, where their enthusiasm could be put to good use. Hayes had to shake his head at himself.

He wasn't an old man, but he sure felt like it sometimes.

"The rest of you come with me," Hayes said. "Chapman, Mason, good hunting."

TWENTY-FIVE

Clint and Allison stepped into the alley and immediately divided it in half. Clint started walking slowly along the left side while Allison took the right. Neither of them said a word as they carefully studied every scrape in the dirt and each pile of crates or paper they found.

Every one of their senses was being pushed to its limit, and it was bad enough that their ears were still ringing a bit from the recent gunfire.

As he took small steps down his side of the alley, Clint went over everything he knew that might be of any help in tracking down the killer he was after. He didn't have to walk too far to realize that he knew next to nothing of any real value.

All he knew for certain was that a girl had been brutally killed and that she wasn't the first. He also knew that she wouldn't be the last. He'd seen too much of man's foul nature to believe any different.

The way the girl was killed and left behind showed that the killer wasn't just some bloodthirsty animal. A certain amount of patience and skill was needed to do what had been done to Mary Swann. That much skill only came to a man who loved his line of work.

That thought put Clint into an even darker mood simply because he knew it was true. The darkness lifted a bit, however, when he caught the glint of metal on the ground.

"Lookee here," Clint said while squatting down.

Allison stepped up beside him and hunkered down as well so she could get a closer look. "What is it? What did you find?"

Reaching out with one hand, Clint picked up something and then held it between his thumb and forefinger. "Looks like a rifle cartridge." He brought the piece of blackened copper to his nose and took a quick sniff. "And it wasn't fired that long ago."

"Are you sure about that?" Allison asked excitedly.

"Pretty sure."

"And you know it's from a rifle?"

There were plenty of different things Clint could have pointed out to prove that, ranging from the fairly obvious to subtle matters that only came from crafting guns for so many years. Rather than get into any of that, however, he simply nodded and said, "Yep. I'm certain about it."

"That's good enough for me." After shifting in her spot, Allison suddenly let out another anxious sound. "And look here. Boot prints."

Clint glanced to where she was pointing, but didn't allow himself to get too worked up over what he saw. "Can you see where they came from?"

"They go back into the alley a ways." She stood up and walked back there herself. Before too long at all, she stopped and made a few circles while studying the ground. She wound up facing Clint one more time with a shrug. "They stop here. Actually, they blend more into the rest of the tracks that come and go through here."

"Including ours."

"Yeah. Including ours."

"I didn't really expect to find much by way of tracks

around here. Chances are they'd just lead back out to a street before joining up with another couple hundred sets that look just like them."

"So, you're a tracker as well as a shooter and a gun-smith?" Allison asked. "I'm impressed."

Clint straightened up and dusted off his knee. "No need to be. That's all pretty much just common sense. Something tells me that you wish you could see which street those tracks lead to so you could trace down every last set of prints you found there."

"What makes you say that?"

"The fire in your eyes. The last time I saw something like it was in a bloodhound that was tied up to a post after catching a fresh scent."

"I'm not sure I like being compared to a dog, but I guess that's not too far off the mark. I didn't get this far in tracking down this son of a bitch being pointed by anyone else. Since I'm not exactly an expert tracker, I use whatever I can to get what I need. And if that means following up on every last footprint I can find, then so be it."

"Well, there's nothing wrong with that," Clint said. "Just make sure you point all that effort in the right direction."

"How?"

"By finding the rifle that fired this round," he replied, holding up the spent casing. "By the way people reacted to what happened out there, gunfights aren't that common in this town. And since the powder on this shell is still pretty fresh . . ."

"Whoever shot it is probably the man we're after," Allison finished.

"More than likely." Clint was about to say something else when he cut himself short.

Allison had no trouble in picking up on the way Clint's ears pricked up and his eyes snapped back toward the other end of the alley. Her gun hand flashed down toward her

holster, only to find it empty. She immediately began looking around and didn't stop until she spotted a hunk of broken lumber propped up against a wall.

With a quick motion, she took hold of the lumber and
gripped it tightly with both hands. Once she was wielding
her makeshift club, she looked back to Clint. Allison's
heart skipped a beat when she realized that Clint was no
longer in the spot where he'd been a moment ago.

Before she could make a noise or even whisper his
name, Clint poked his head out from behind the stack of
crates where he'd taken up his new position. He'd moved
from one spot to another like a shadow gliding over a wall.

Once he saw that he'd silenced her, he pointed toward
the other end of the alley. After she nodded back to him,
Clint motioned for her to stay put. He didn't wait to see if
she would actually stay in one place or not. Instead, Clint
kept his back to one wall while moving toward the noise
he'd heard.

He was almost close enough to pounce on whoever had
been trying to sneak up on them when Clint saw someone
step out from another stack of crates. Every one of Clint's
muscles tensed when he saw the man was carrying a gun.

TWENTY-SIX

"Looking for this?" Jeremiah asked as he held up a rifle in one hand.

"Jesus Christ," Clint said as he let out the breath that had been building up inside of him like a head of steam. "I could've hurt you sneaking up on me like that. What the hell are you doing here?"

Allison rushed down the alley and skidded to a stop when she saw that Clint was in no danger. She had a similar surprised look on her face when she got a look at who Clint was talking to. "Jeremiah? Is that you?"

"Of course it is. Who were you expecting?"

"Not you," she replied. "What are you doing here?"

The blacksmith regarded each of them with a small measure of annoyance in his eyes. "I don't answer to either of you, no matter what you might think. And I'm not about to sit in my shop and go on like nothing happened."

Clint could smell the whiskey on the man's breath and heard the subtle slur to his words. He knew it wouldn't accomplish much to call the man on it. In fact, considering all that had happened, he couldn't really blame him.

"What are you doing with that rifle?" Clint asked.

Jeremiah held onto the rifle by its barrel, allowing the

rest of the weapon to hang down from his fist. He extended his arm toward Clint and said, "It's not mine. I found it here in this alley not too far from where you two were poking around."

"Did you know about what happened earlier?" Allison asked.

"The fight? Of course I knew. They're talking about it all over town. Hell, I could hear the shots from my shop."

Clint made sure to keep his eyes focused on the man. As far as he could tell, Jeremiah might have had a drink or two, but he wasn't drunk by any stretch of the imagination. "What were you doing in this alley, Jeremiah?"

"Same thing you were. I heard about what happened and that someone took a shot at you from around here."

"How'd you know about that?" Allison asked. "We barely got that much out of anyone and we were in the middle of everything."

"Because folks around here know me," Jeremiah said simply. "They told me everything they knew because I'm not some gunfighter from out of town or an unfamiliar face."

"Still," Clint said. "Sneaking around here isn't exactly the brightest idea, you know."

"If I was sneaking, Mr. Adams, I wouldn't have announced myself to you both like I did."

For a moment, Clint came up short on what to say. All he could manage before things got too awkward was "Good point."

Jeremiah nodded once and held the rifle out to Clint one more time. "Here. Take this if this is what you're after. I can be a help to you in this or I can go about it my own way. Whichever it is, I won't be pushed aside like some child while the adults go about their work."

"I'll keep that in mind," Clint said as he accepted the rifle. "But keep in mind that you're not exactly accustomed to dealing with killers. Taking a wrong step in this could be just as dangerous as if I walked into your shop and started throwing around hot metal without knowing what the hell I was doing."

Jeremiah looked at Clint and nodded before too long. "You're right. Just let me lend a hand wherever I can. Please."

"You got it." Only then did Clint start to examine the rifle he'd taken from Jeremiah. He opened the breech and took a look inside before sniffing once at the slot where spent cartridges were expelled.

"Is that the rifle we wanted?" Allison asked.

The only reason Clint paused was that he hadn't been the one to find the rifle himself. A skeptical part of him knew only too well that Jeremiah could have brought that rifle in from anywhere. Then again, if he was going to work with the blacksmith, they would have to start by trusting one another.

"Yep," Clint replied. "Looks like this is it."

TWENTY-SEVEN

"Yep," the small man said with a nod of his head. "It's Indian, all right."

Dell was still breathing heavily after all the unexpected activity of finding and dealing with the fight that had exploded farther in town. Now that he'd dealt with Clint Adams as well as handed over two more bodies to the town's undertaker, the deputy still felt his heart fluttering inside his chest.

"So an Injun definitely put them marks there?" Dell asked.

Ernie Niedelander seemed tiny compared to the deputy, but that was mostly because he was practically on his belly on the ground. Without taking his eyes off the root that had been pointed out to him, he straightened up and worked some kinks out of his knees. "I didn't say that."

"You did so. I just heard you."

"No. What I said was that the mark itself is Indian. I have no way of telling whether or not an actual Indian put it there. You or I could very well have scratched that mark into there just as easily as an Indian could have."

Although Dell wanted to argue the point some more, he knew that the other man was right. Ernie Niedelander was a thin, scholarly looking man who wore rounded spectacles on the bridge of a pointy nose. He was seldom seen in anything but a brown suit that was in desperate need of stitching. Beaten shoes covered awkward feet in much the same way that his rumpled hair covered a bulbous head.

Ernie had been of service to the sheriff a few times and had become sort of a local expert on many things. That didn't mean that Ernie was so smart, but he did know more than most folks about obscure facts and figures.

"Do you know what it means?" Dell asked.

Ernie looked down at the root and cocked his head. Even though he'd been staring at the mark scratched there for a few minutes now, he seemed to take it in from a slightly different perspective every time he readjusted his feet.

"That depends on which way is up," Ernie said.

"What?"

"Well, if it was meant to be seen the way we're looking at it now, it might be a Navajo symbol. If it was carved from the opposite direction, for example by someone standing over here . . ." As he said this, Ernie walked around the stump so that he was facing Dell with the root between them. "From here, it might be of Cherokee origin."

Dell shook his head, partly from frustration and partly from confusion. "Do you know what it means or not?"

Looking back at the deputy while struggling to put his thoughts together, Ernie finally nodded. "You see, that's the odd part. No matter how you look at it, the symbol really doesn't make sense. I mean, it does, but not in this context."

Dell didn't need to say a word. The expression on his face was similar to that of a dog trying to figure out how a clock worked. Ernie could feel the tension building within the other man's skull from where he stood.

"All right," Ernie said. "It can mean one of two things. From where you're standing, it could be a symbol representing a harvest festival. Or from where I'm standing, it could be the symbol for one of a few spirit totems."

"That spirit one could be it," Dell said quickly. "Maybe she's being marked because of her spirit. Or that her spirit is gone now. You know, since she's dead."

Ernie listened to the deputy with patience, but didn't share one bit of the hopeful enthusiasm in Dell's voice. Instead, he waited until the deputy was finished talking before wincing slightly and shrugging.

"I guess that's possible," Ernie said.

Letting out a breath, Dell looked back down at the mark scratched into the root. "No, you don't," he muttered. "And neither do I. Jesus, what the hell am I supposed to tell the sheriff? He's already going to be pissed to know that I was out here waiting for you when anther gunfight broke out in town."

"Sorry I was late. It was kind of hard not to get swept up in that fight when it happened. I heard the shots and just—"

"No need for any of that," Dell said. "I just wish this carving meant something. It seemed important, and by God, I just know it was put here for a reason."

"Oh, it's important," Ernie said with confidence. "And it was put here for a reason. We just need to figure out what the reason is. Once we do that, we'll be closer to what everyone's after." He glanced over to the stump itself and the bloodstains which had become black patterns within the bark. "We'll be closer to the sick animal that spilled so much innocent blood."

TWENTY-EIGHT

Even though the days tended to grow shorter as the wind grew colder, this day seemed even shorter than most. Before Clint had a chance to look at his pocket watch, the sun was already dipping below the horizon and the light coming through his window was getting more and more faint.

Not that Clint took much notice of it, however. He'd been holed up in the same room for all of the afternoon as well as the early evening. More than that, he was hunched down over the same table for most of that time. His hands remained busy and his mind was focused on the simple task he'd taken on.

Allison had been coming and going, checking in on him every now and then, in between tending to her own affairs. She brought some food and water, but mostly kept to herself.

That just left Jeremiah. He was never far from Clint's sight throughout this time. Of course, that was only to be expected since Clint was taking up space within Jeremiah's shop.

"Taking another drink, Jeremiah?" Clint asked without looking up from his work.

Jeremiah's arm was cocked upward, lifting the bottle to

his mouth. He stayed frozen there for a moment before finally lifting the bottle the rest of the way so he could pour some firewater down his throat. Swallowing with a grateful sigh, he set the bottle down.

"Yeah, I'm taking a drink. You want some?"

Clint shook his head. "Never really cared for the stuff. I'd just hate for you to keel over at the wrong time."

The laugh Jeremiah let out wasn't much more than a grunt. "Wrong time? Since my little girl turned up butchered, there ain't no more right times in my life. I suspect that's how it will always be."

Reaching out for another tool, Clint put it to use and glanced up at the blacksmith as his hands went about their task. "It hasn't been that long."

Blinking, Jeremiah said, "Feels like it's been years." He blinked a few more times, shook his head and took another sip from the bottle. "It feels like years since you started pulling that gun apart. Are you ever going to be done with that?"

The rifle Jeremiah had found was spread out on a table in front of Clint like a body from a medical text. A large cloth covered the table at the back of the blacksmith's shack, on top of which were laying each individual piece of the rifle.

"Actually," Clint said while separating three pieces and then setting aside the tool he'd been using. "I'm done right now."

Jeremiah walked over to look down at what Clint had done. "Did you find out anything?"

"Not as much as I would've liked. First of all, there's this." As he said that, he picked up the wooden stock and turned it around so the bottom edge was facing up. Tracing his finger along the grain, he stopped at a nick in the wood and said, "See that mark?"

Squinting down through the whiskey haze and the fading light in the room, Jeremiah finally nodded. "Yeah. Looks like a cut or a groove."

"It's too small to be made from dropping it and too fresh to have been there for more than a few days. I'd say it's a notch made by a knife."

"A notch? You mean like a gunfighter uses?"

"Some gunfighters use them. I'd say it's marking off the man that was killed in front of me and Allison."

"How does that help?"

"It tells me that the shooter is the kind that likes to keep track of his kills. That's not as common as you might think. And I think he plans on using this gun again."

"Really? Where d'you see that?"

"More of a gut instinct," Clint replied. "I didn't find much of anything in the pieces, but taking this rifle apart showed me something. You see these parts?" he asked, nodding toward all the bits of metal and wood spread out before him. "They're cleaner and better maintained than most guns are when they're new."

Jeremiah kept squinting down at them. "Clean's clean to me."

"This rifle's more than clean. It's been tended and cared for by a loving hand." Clint gazed down at the disassembled rifle with an appreciation that only someone familiar to his craft would feel. "It's not the sort of thing someone would use once and toss away."

"So do you think it was the killer who used that rifle?" Jeremiah asked.

"I couldn't be certain."

"What's your gut tell you?"

Clint paused for a moment before answering. He did so mainly to decide if he wanted to say the words that had already come to mind. "Yeah," he said before too much longer. "I'd say anyone who took the time to care for a weapon like this and make a shot as skilled as the one that killed that man today has a flair for killing. I think that's the man we're after."

"So why would he leave a gun like that just laying

around?" Jeremiah asked. "Especially since he thinks so highly of it."

"He probably just didn't want to be seen with it. I mean, if he's been doing this for long enough, he must know how to go about it without getting caught."

Jeremiah's face took on a cold harshness. "Yeah. He's real good at that."

"He at least knows better than to be seen running away from a shooting carrying a smoking rifle. But there's at least one thing we know for certain," Clint added.

"What's that?"

"He'll want his rifle back." Looking back down to the pieces in front of him, Clint grabbed a different tool and got to work. "And that might just be the very opening we've been waiting for."

TWENTY-NINE

By the time Clint got back to his room, the sky was darker than pitch. It was the thick kind of blackness that only seemed to fill an autumn or winter sky, and it came with just as much cold as one might expect for that time of year.

Reaching out for the handle to his door, Clint found that it moved freely. That sent a chill through him since he was certain that he'd locked his door the last time he'd been there. His hand moved reflexively as he pushed open the door and stepped inside.

Allison was waiting there for him, sitting in the room's only chair with a casual smile on her face. "I was beginning to wonder when you might come back." She stood up and walked toward him. "Then I started to hope that you might have been at my room looking for me."

"Actually, that was my next stop," Clint replied.

"Well now," she said, looking down below his belt. "There's a surprise."

Clint's hand was at hip level. He was holding the Colt New Line which he'd drawn in a flash the moment he realized that someone was in his room. Now that he was inside and could see there was nobody apart from Allison, he lowered the gun.

"And what about that rifle?" she asked as she drew up closer to him. "Did you have any luck there?"

"Maybe. We'll just have to wait and see what develops."

Allison was close enough to Clint now that they could feel the heat coming from each other's body. Although she reached out for him with both hands, she kept from touching him. Instead, she savored being so close to him before fully giving in to what she wanted.

Clint could feel her hands brushing over him. Suddenly, the air didn't seem so cold and he was able to set aside the blood and death that had soaked into him over the last few days.

"He's still out there, isn't he?" Allison said.

Clint nodded. "He's not going anywhere. After all the dust he's kicked up, the last thing he'll want is to go before things finish up. But there's nothing we can do about it right now."

"There's always something to be done." Even as she said that, she allowed herself to move against him a bit more, pressing herself slowly against Clint's chest. "I've learned that the hard way."

Clint could feel the muscles in Allison's back start to relax. It wasn't until that moment that he realized how tightly wound she'd been. Compared to the way she felt against him at that moment, she'd been spending the rest of the time with her fists clenched and her shoulders up around her ears.

With just a little caress along her back, Clint felt her relax even more. Finally, she let out a contented sigh and moved her hands over him. Suddenly, Clint realized he was relaxing as well, like a pain that had been around for so long that he only realized it had been there once it stopped.

"We must be a sight," she whispered. "Right now it feels like we're the only things holding each other up."

Clint placed a finger under her chin and lifted her face so she was looking up at him. Allison's eyes were the color of smooth leather and her skin felt like silk. The way she looked up at him was both trusting and expectant.

Forgetting what he was going to say, Clint let his actions speak for him and leaned down to kiss her on the lips.

The kiss was more like them melting together. Both of them tensed for a brief moment, but quickly let that go when they felt just how much the other had wanted that very moment to come. In no time at all, their hands were moving over each other's body, plunging under shirts, pulling open buttons, doing anything they could to feel bare skin.

Moaning under her breath, Allison returned Clint's kiss with a passion that grew by the second. Her lips practically devoured him, and even that wasn't enough to satisfy the need burning inside of her. As her hands pulled at Clint's clothes, she opened her mouth to taste him even more, allowing her tongue to slip inside his mouth.

Clint's body reacted instantly to her. Already, his erection was pushing against his jeans. And even though he was grateful to feel that tension relieved, he was a little surprised at the same time. He'd barely felt a tug at his belt before Allison's hands had worked their way between his legs.

She squirmed and writhed against him, easing herself out of her clothes as soon as Clint loosened them, while also easing her way closer to him. Once her fingers grazed against the bare skin of his stomach, she worked her way down until she finally got hold of his rigid penis.

Now it was Clint's turn to let out a sigh as he felt her fingers encircle his cock and start stroking gently back and forth. Her mouth was still pressed tightly against his own, every one of Allison's breaths sounding like a torrent since she was so close to him.

Allison's shirt hung open and her jeans dropped down around her ankles so she could kick them to another part of the room. When she felt Clint's hand move along her inner thigh, she opened her legs just enough for him to reach in and touch the warmth between them.

The smooth lips of her vagina were damp and hot to the touch. They parted like flower petals for Clint's fingers, and when he started to rub them, Allison finally broke their kiss and leaned back.

The breath she let out then was long, slow and shuddering. She savored every movement of his fingers until finally her eyes snapped open and her breath started to come in short, shallow gulps.

Clint could see the approaching orgasm in her eyes. When it came, it was just enough to make her bite down on her bottom lip while grinding against his hand. It passed in a few seconds, leaving her gasping for breath.

"Come on," she whispered while taking his hand and leading Clint to the bed. "We've got a long night ahead of us."

THIRTY

Allison's hands were strong and insistent as she led Clint to the bed. Once they got there, Clint took over and grabbed hold of her by the shoulders. She let out a surprised little breath as her eyes got wide. Even so, she was more than happy to let herself be moved to wherever Clint wanted to place her.

Positioning her against the foot of the bed, Clint slid his hands down along her sides as he lowered himself down to his knees. Allison lowered herself as well, until she was sitting on the edge of the bed's frame. Once there, she spread her legs open and leaned back as Clint kissed a line down her stomach to the soft thatch of hair between her thighs.

Leaning back even farther, Allison propped herself up with both arms. Her long hair flowed back to brush against the mattress as she started to sway back and forth while letting out a quiet moan. Clint's lips grazed against the bare skin of her legs. Their clothes had come off somewhere between where they'd started and where they'd wound up, in a way that made it seem as if they'd melted off their bodies.

Clint kept his hands on Allison's skin, savoring the smooth softness of it. The more he worked his mouth on

117

her, the warmer her skin became under his palms. Before too long, he could feel her trembling slightly with anticipation as his lips moved closer and closer to the wet lips of her pussy. When he finally opened his mouth and let his tongue flick against her inner thigh, she flinched and wriggled against his face.

"Oh yes," she purred. "Right there."

The room was almost completely dark. By this time, however, Clint's eyes had had enough time to adjust to the shadows. He was able to make out the trim lines of her body as she wriggled and squirmed in front of him. Her taut belly trembled with every breath, and her large breasts swayed gently as the nipples became rigid little nubs.

"Oh God, Clint," Allison groaned as she reached out to grab the back of his head. "Right there. That's so good."

Allison's fingers threaded through his hair, holding Clint in position while her hips started to press against his probing mouth. Clint took hold of her hips in his hands and tightened his own grip as well. He could tell the moment his tongue had found a sweet spot by the way her breathing picked up and her pussy became even wetter against his lips.

Surprisingly, Clint felt Allison tugging his head upward even as she let out a loud, pleasurable moan. As much as he wanted to stay where he was, Clint let himself be taken from between her legs so he could move his mouth up along the supple curves of her torso. When he looked up, Clint found Allison looking right back at him. The hungry look in her eyes was more than enough to make his cock even more rigid and ready for her.

Despite the fact that her hands had slipped and were moving up and down his body, Clint didn't need any more guidance to know what she wanted. Allison's body writhed against him, and her face was twisted into an expression of intense desire.

Clint settled on top of her, taking in the sight of Allison's naked body underneath him. She arched her back to push her proud, solid breasts against him. When he moved one hand up along her to brush his thumb against her nipple, Clint felt a response run through her entire body. Her legs tightened around him and she started to grind her wet pussy against the shaft of his penis.

Now it was Clint's turn to arch his back and savor the pleasure he was being given. The wet lips between Allison's legs moved up and down along his cock, massaging his erection until he practically ached to be inside of her.

When he shifted to try and do that very thing, Clint found himself grinding against her even more. It seemed that she was trying to keep him where he was for the moment, and Clint might have gotten flustered if it didn't feel so damn good.

Before too long, Clint couldn't take it any longer. He opened his eyes and fixed his gaze upon her. Allison was breathing heavily and almost glaring back at him. When he guided himself into her and thrust his hips forward, Clint saw her eyes widen and felt every one of her muscles practically jump beneath her skin.

Clint's hands rubbed against every part of her he could reach. He wound up with one hand grabbing her leg and the other clasping hold of her tight buttocks. From there, he could guide every one of her motions as he began pumping between her legs.

Having surrendered herself to him, Allison leaned back and let herself be controlled by Clint's powerful body. Her legs opened for him and she wrapped one arm around his shoulders. Her other arm switched between grabbing the edge of the mattress and sliding a hand through her hair.

Allison's mouth opened, but no sound came out. With Clint's rigid cock filling her, all she could do was try and catch her breath while moans of pleasure became lodged in her throat. Soon, she felt both of his hands take hold of her backside, lifting her up off the bed as he moved in closer.

Raising himself onto his knees, Clint scooted onto the bed while easing Allison closer to the headboard. He then scooped her up and positioned her just right without once allowing himself to slip out of her. In one motion, he pulled her to him while pumping his hips forward, driving his rigid penis all the way inside of her.

Allison not only found her voice, but was able to unleash all the groans that had been building up inside of her the entire time. After letting out that first groan, her lips formed a satisfied smile as they curled around every other sound that came out of her.

"Yes, Clint! Do it harder!" she cried.

Clint was only too happy to oblige.

As his thrusts became more and more powerful, the bed started rocking back and forth underneath them both. Allison reached up to hold on to the headboard as she arched her back and wriggled her hips back and forth in his hands.

"That's the way," she groaned. "God, yes!"

After one more thrust, Clint set her down and allowed himself to come out of her. When he saw Allison's expression turn into a disappointed frown, he smirked and pulled in a deep breath.

"Don't worry," he said between heaving breaths. "I'm not done with you yet."

After saying that, Clint reached down to slide one hand beneath her neck so he could lift her up and plant a kiss onto her waiting mouth. When he let her go, he took hold of her hips one more time. Feeling his hands upon her was enough for Allison to open her legs and lift her hips up toward him one more time. But Clint had something else in mind.

Shaking his head, Clint smiled mischievously and used his hands to flip her over. Although the motion was a little unexpected, Allison was smiling broadly by the time her breasts hit the mattress. In a matter of seconds, she'd quickly repositioned her legs and was lifting her backside up for him expectantly.

Clint took a moment to catch his breath, as well as to get a look at the beautiful sight in front of him. Allison's body was a smooth landscape of flowing curves and glorious possibilities. Her spine stretched up in a gentle slope which disappeared beneath the wild tangle of her hair. Her backside was firm and pointed upward to display the wet lips that he'd come to know so well.

It seemed that Clint's body moved of its own accord, because he was sliding between her thighs before he was done admiring her figure. The moment he felt the tip of his penis press against that warm, moist pussy, he let his instincts take over.

They both let out a pleasured moan as Clint slid all the way inside of her, until his hips pressed against the soft curve of her buttocks. Clint reached out with both hands to slide along her back, massaging the muscles there while working his way upward. Once he got hold of her shoulders, he tightened his grip and began pounding in and out.

Allison tossed her head back, whipping her hair against Clint's forearms. She quickly found his rhythm and complemented it by rocking herself back and forth in time to his thrusts. The sway of her breasts combined with the feel of him inside of her sent chills through her flesh. Soon, she felt the stirrings of another climax within her.

Although the first one had been good, this one had her moaning instantly. Clint could feel what he was doing to her in the way she began bucking against him. Even the lips of her pussy tightened around him, bringing him even closer to his own pinnacle.

Allison's moans became louder and louder before they were cut off altogether. Soon she was feeling so much pleasure that she couldn't make another sound to express it. Instead, she clenched her eyes shut and balled her fists until her orgasm had swept through every last part of her body.

Clint pumped a few more times before he felt his own toes start to curl. Grabbing hold of her tightly, he thrust one last time before exploding inside of her. Only then was he able to let go of the breath he'd been holding and finally relax his grip upon her hips.

He stayed inside of her for a few seconds, savoring the way her wet lips folded around his erection. When he felt that his hands were the only thing holding her up, Clint slipped out of her and let go so they could both drop onto the bed in an exhausted heap.

The room seemed to be swirling around him as Clint lay his head onto the pillow. Although there was a chill in the air, that was soon taken away by the heat of Allison's body as she curled up beside him. She draped one arm across his chest and slipped the other under his head before nestling her head on his shoulder.

Clint slipped one arm under the pillows, but stopped short before wrapping it around her. His hand had touched against something that nearly caused him to say something out loud. The only thing that kept him quiet was that he'd immediately recognized what he'd found.

It was a gun.

It wasn't a big gun, but the fact that it was there at all made him wonder about a whole lot of things.

There was always the possibility that it had been left there by someone who'd been in the room before Clint had rented it, but that seemed unlikely since Clint had been staying there for a few days. The chances of him missing a gun under his pillow were zero, which left only the possibility that it had been placed there by someone else.

The only other person to be in Clint's bed that he knew of was the contented woman now resting in his arms. After a few subtle adjustments, Clint's arm snaked out from under the pillow and wrapped around Allison. He soon fell into a welcome, although light, sleep.

THIRTY-ONE

The campfire crackled in the darkness like a single star twinkling in a sea of black. Once the sun had dropped below the horizon, the shadows had become thick as ink. There was some wind churning, but it was slow and cumbersome, heavy with cold.

Mason and Chapman sat around that fire, holding their hands out and rubbing them without much success. They felt just enough of the flame's warmth to keep their teeth from chattering, but not enough to keep the rest of them from shaking under the layers of clothes they wore.

"Jesus H. Christ, it is cold," Mason said. "I swear I got ice runnin' through my veins right about now."

Chapman had twisted around to open the pack that he'd been leaning against. After a few moments of rummaging, he pulled his hand back out to show a bottle of whiskey. Opening it, he said, "This ought to help a bit."

The whiskey poured down his throat and worked its way through his body. Closing his eyes and letting out a breath, the deputy could feel every drop of the liquor warm him from the inside out as it traced its curving path down into his gullet.

Mason was already reaching out with one hand like a kid eager to take hold of a sarsaparilla. "Hand it over!"

Chapman did just that and then reached his palms out toward the fire one more time. He could hear the loud gulps coming from the other side of the fire, followed by a wheezing sigh.

"That's the stuff," Mason said. "How long were you plannin' on holding on to this?"

"Sal gave it to me before we left. After all the times I kept that saloon of his open throughout the years, he figured he owes me. Tell you the truth, I almost forgot the bottle was there."

"Well, I'm sure glad you remembered," Mason said before tipping back the bottle one more time and handing it back.

Although he wasn't about to drink as much as his partner, Chapman was set to take a bit more of the cold out of his system when he stopped short. The bottle was halfway to his mouth and even dripped a little onto the front of his shirt as he turned to look away from the fire. "What was that?"

Mason glanced around before looking back to Chapman. "What was what?"

Neither man made a noise.

The only thing that could be heard was the crackle of the fire.

The only thing that moved was the shadows thrown by the dancing flames.

Finally, Chapman twitched. "That. Right there. Didn't you hear it?"

Mason froze. Every now and then his eyes would shift in their sockets, but his muscles had become as unmoving as rock. "I can't hear anything."

"Well, I did," Chapman replied. He'd already set the bottle down and was reaching back for the shotgun nearby. "Something's moving out there."

"I can't see anything."

"That's because we're here by this fire and everything around us is in the dark. I thought you were the goddamn hunter, for Christ's sake."

"Aw hell," Mason grumbled as he drew the pistol that had been holstered at his side. "There's always something moving out there."

Chapman didn't bother explaining himself to the other man. He could already see Mason pulling himself together and turning toward the sound that he supposedly hadn't heard. Part of him couldn't blame the other man for not wanting to leave the fire and whiskey. Another part of him was wishing he hadn't taken that drink for himself.

Already, Chapman could feel the little bit of sluggishness from the few gulps of firewater he'd taken. It wasn't much, but it was enough to make him extra careful as he wandered out of the firelight. When he heard the definite sound of something heavier than a rabbit walking in the shadows, the beating of his heart shook Chapman out of any effects he might have felt from the whiskey.

Mason had heard it, too. He looked back to the deputy, nodded, and pointed in the direction the sound had come from. After a few more quickly exchanged signals, both lawmen hunched down low and moved off in separate directions.

The more Chapman moved through the darkness, the more his eyes became accustomed to it. His hands clenched around his shotgun and he started picking out more shapes in the shadows.

Every now and then, something moved, but it was a small skittering that was hard to pin down. Before he could write off the sounds as nothing, they became heavier and more deliberate.

Something was definitely out there, he knew.

Actually, more of a someone.

Mason was getting that same feeling as well. Once he got a quick look at the area around him, he began circling back so he could cover Chapman. As far as he could tell, the other deputy was covering himself well enough by keeping his back to a tree or rocks whenever possible. But it was impossible to watch your own back for too long.

That was what partners were for, and Mason wasn't about to shirk his duty in that respect.

Mason saw his partner moving toward another crackle of breaking twigs. Deciding to work his way around to cover Chapman's blind spot, Mason heard a rustle coming from behind him.

Casually, Mason turned to look at the whisper of a sound and found himself staring into a set of wide, intense eyes. The glint of metal flickered at the edge of his field of vision right before he felt a solid thump against his torso followed by the pain of steel raking against his ribs.

"You looking for me?" came a voice that was a rasping snarl in Mason's ear. "Looks like you found me. Let's see how long it takes for someone to find you."

A hand had clamped over Mason's mouth, suppressing his startled scream as the blade was pulled from his gut and raked along the top of his forehead.

THIRTY-TWO

Chapman heard sounds coming from Mason's direction, but pushed them to the back of his mind so he could focus on the other sounds that had brought him away from the fire in the first place. The farther out he got, however, the more a grim realization began to take hold in him.

There was nothing to be found. At least, there was nothing where he was looking.

It had only been a matter of seconds, but each one of those had stretched out like hours in his mind. He was so busy looking at every movement he could find and hearing every rustle of the wind against the ground that it had taken him a while to realize how little was out there.

Whatever he'd heard before, Chapman now knew it had been a distraction. That grim realization sank like a cold rock inside his stomach and caused him to spin around while bringing up his gun.

"Mason?" Chapman said to the shadows. "Where are you?"

The deputy's steps became quick and scrambled against the dirt. His eyes tried to look in every direction at once as his pistol searched for a target. Soon the sound of racing footsteps reached his ears.

127

"Mason! What's going on?"

But Chapman's words went unanswered. That didn't keep him from moving on, however, as the deputy quickly found himself back at the spot where he'd made camp.

The fire was still crackling and the horses were still milling about nearby. Having been staring so intently into the darkness, Chapman's eyes were put through a terrible strain when they snapped back around to take in the sight of the campfire.

Looking directly at those flames stung him as if he'd accidentally looked up into the sun. Squinting through the glaring flames while slowing to avoid tripping over their supplies, Chapman did his level best to keep himself moving in his best guess as to where the other lawman had gone.

Stopping himself before shouting for Mason one more time, Chapman swallowed hard and strained his senses to catch any trace of his partner. His efforts were soon rewarded as he made out a few shapes not too far from the light of the fire.

The one shape that caught his attention the most was what appeared to be the outline of a small man crouching down close to the ground. Both of the figure's arms were tucked in close to its body, and its head seemed to be waggling like the tail of a dog.

In no time at all, Chapman realized that the figure he'd seen wasn't exactly small and waggling. It was actually far away and running quickly to get even farther. Chapman's legs started working furiously to catch up to the figure, but in another second the figure had disappeared from sight altogether.

Before he could follow, Chapman heard a pained voice and nearly slipped in a slick patch of dirt. The mud nearly took his foot out from under him as the deputy struggled to regain his balance. Just as he was about to right himself, he damn near tripped over a prone body.

"Mason?" Chapman said as he dropped down to get a look at the figure on the ground. "Aw, Jesus."

Mason was struggling to push himself off the ground using his elbows, but only succeeded in lifting his back an inch or two before dropping down again.

After just having reached down to steady the other lawman, Chapman could feel that Mason's shirt was wet with freshly spilled blood. "Don't try to move," he said, doing his best to keep his voice calm and collected. "You're hurt."

"Not . . . not hurt," Mason gurgled. "I'm dyin'."

Chapman's first instinct was to dent that claim, if only to keep the other man's spirits up. But denying those words right then would have been like denying that the sky was over their heads. "Who did this to you?" Chapman asked instead. "Where'd he go?"

"Don' know," Mason said. "He's the one we're after. Forget me an' go get him."

Letting out a breath, Chapman nodded grimly and set the other deputy gently back onto the ground. He had to fight back the impulse to take off running after the killer, so he could get to his horse instead. Rather than waste time saddling up the animal, Chapman climbed onto its bare back and dug his heels into the massive ribs.

One of Chapman's hands was clenched around a chunk of his horse's mane while the other was wrapped tightly around his gun. He thundered in the direction he'd last spotted that other figure, hoping that either God or the Devil would help him find the son of a bitch.

At that moment, Chapman didn't care which one answered him.

THIRTY-THREE

The sunlight beaming through the window marked the beginning of another day. Clint didn't bring up the topic of the gun he'd found under the pillow the night before. He even kept it to himself when he discovered the gun had gone missing come morning.

Allison was up and pulling on her shirt when Clint opened his eyes. She'd managed to do all of that without him being any the wiser. Considering how lightly he'd forced himself to sleep, that was no small feat. But he kept that to himself as well.

Choking back so much at the start of the day wasn't as hard as it might have sounded. Judging by the pounding which suddenly erupted from his door, Clint would have more than enough to occupy his mind.

"What the hell is that?" he grumbled as he hopped out of bed and pulled on the clothes he could reach.

"Sounds like we'll be skipping breakfast," Allison said with a smirk that didn't go well with the increasingly violent pounding on the door.

Clint reached for his boots. "You think this is so funny, then you can answer it," he said.

Turning toward the door, Allison stepped forward and said, "Maybe I will."

Clint took note of the way her hand drifted toward the back side of her right hip. Since she was obviously not merely straightening her belt, he guessed that he'd discovered the likeliest place the missing gun could be found. He kept that to himself as well, as he stepped toward the door while gently moving Allison out of his way.

"Get back," Clint said. "And don't get too jumpy."

Before the door could get pounded off its hinges, Clint opened it. All he had to do was work the latch and the next knock did the rest of his work for him. A fist smacked against the door from the other side, knocking the door against Clint's boot.

Sheriff Hayes stood in the hall with his hand up as if he couldn't decide whether or not he should keep knocking. The lawman's eyes fixed on Clint before darting over both of Clint's shoulders. "You in there alone, Adams?"

"No," Allison replied, beating Clint to the punch. "But the last time I checked, there wasn't a law against that."

Ignoring Allison's words along with the smirk on her face, Sheriff Hayes looked back to Clint and said, "Come on, Adams. It's time for your hearing."

"That was quick."

"Yeah, well, considering the circumstances, Judge Zellner wanted to push things on a bit."

Clint didn't like the sound of that. "What circumstances?"

Hayes studied Clint's face the way he might study a snake threatening to sink its fangs into his leg. "One of my men was killed last night. Looks like it was done by the same son of a bitch that killed the Swann girl."

The smirk on Allison's face disappeared as if it had never even been there. She rushed forward as though she meant to charge right over Clint, the lawman or anyone else who might get in her way. "Where is he? Where did it happen?"

Stopping her with a quickly outstretched hand, Hayes nodded to one of his men. "Take her with us," he said. "Judge's orders."

Although the deputies weren't particularly rough with her, Allison struggled against them with everything she had. That, in turn, forced the deputies to put a little more muscle into their own efforts.

"Allison, stop fighting them," Clint ordered. "You're only making it worse."

"Allison Little?" Sheriff Hayes asked.

Allison stared back at him with bare defiance. "You know who I am."

"I'm gonna need you to come with us as well."

"What? I'm not on trial!"

"The hell you ain't!" one of the deputies spouted.

Hayes held a hand out to the deputy who'd spoken up, which was more than enough to silence him. "You were involved in that shooting yesterday, weren't you?"

"And if there'd been some law around here, maybe none of that would have even happened," she shot back.

Stepping forward, Hayes fixed a glare on her that would have been enough to stop a wild bull in its tracks. "And we were out trying to find a murderer. One of my men was killed by that same bastard a matter of hours ago."

Clint looked back and forth between the two. Although he could feel the tension coming off of Allison like a wave of heat, he was surprised at how quickly the spark had become a flame.

"Adams has to come with us in irons," Hayes said. "But that's only because he's been wrapped up in both dustups. I can take you in the same way or we can all head over to the courthouse nice and civil."

Before Allison had a chance to respond to that, Clint held both arms out with his wrists an inch or so apart. While he was presenting himself to the deputy who had the shackles in his hands, he was also putting himself between

Hayes and Allison. "No need for any of this to get ugly," Clint said. "Put those chains on and let's get this going."

Allison still had plenty of fire in her eyes, but she forced it back and nodded before averting her eyes from the sheriff. The rest of the fight drained out of her once she heard the metallic clatter of the cuffs being fit around Clint's wrists and locked in place. Clint was glad he'd stuck the New Line into his boot rather than his belt.

"This probably doesn't help much right now," Sheriff Hayes said. "But I'll do my best to see this doesn't go too badly for you. I wasn't here for the last fight, but I still don't believe you're the man I'm after, Adams."

"That's good to hear," Clint said. "Let's just hope the judge sees it the same way."

THIRTY-FOUR

The Claymore courthouse wasn't much bigger than the town's school. Although none of the rows of benches taking up most of the back half of the room were empty, attendance wasn't much better than a typical school day either. The docket was full, but that was simply because court was only in session once or twice a month.

By the time Clint and Allison were brought into the courtroom, all of the people present had had more than their share of legal talk and were squirming in their seats. That all changed, however, once the audience turned to see the new prisoners being escorted into the room by a bushel of lawmen.

Judge Zellner wasn't as old as Clint was expecting. In fact, the man didn't look too much older than him. His eyes were sharp as a hawk's and hooded under drooping eyebrows. The thick hair on his head was sprinkled with gray, but it was the lines on his face that made him look wiser and more official than anyone else in the room.

It wasn't anything specific that Clint could put his finger on, but those lines in the judge's face were deep as trenches and jagged as a map that had been scratched into the sand.

Right away, Clint took a liking to this judge. He knew he'd find out real quickly if his instincts were right.

"Guilty," Zellner said with a solid pound from his gavel.

As the hammer smacked against the side of the judge's desk, Clint and Allison couldn't help but flinch.

"Now let's get on with the next case."

Clint let out his breath once he saw the defendant from the previous trial being led out by a single deputy. Since that last pronouncement was actually meant for this fellow, the defendant looked twice as downtrodden as Clint had felt a moment ago.

"Is this the Clint Adams that I've been hearing so much about?" Judge Zellner asked.

Sheriff Hayes nodded. "It is, Your Honor."

Zellner glanced down at a stack of papers in front of him, flipped through until he got to the right ones and then took a moment to glance them over. He nodded and looked back up to find that the lawmen as well as both people in their custody had found their places and were sitting like ducks in a row.

"This is in regards to the shootings that have been turning this once-peaceful community into another Dodge City," Zellner said with disdain.

Once again, Hayes nodded. "It is, Your Honor."

"Then speak your piece and tell me something I don't already know."

Hayes went into a short account of what had happened, giving mostly facts and figures regarding shots fired, who'd been hurt and who'd been killed. He then signaled to one of his deputies, who brought forward the two men who'd been injured that night in Kylie's when Jeremiah Swann had stormed the saloon with a shotgun.

Clint had almost forgotten about those two men, but was plenty glad they were there once they started talking. It didn't take long for them to say what they wanted to say and be shoved back down into their chairs by the deputies.

"Is Mr. Swann here?" Zellner asked.

"I am," came a voice from the audience.

Clint turned around and spotted the blacksmith getting up with his hands clasped in front of him. But it wasn't Joseph that kept Clint's attention. There was another man sitting just behind and to the left of the blacksmith who stood out like a sore thumb.

The man had skin the color of tanned leather, with long hair that was black as a crow's wing. He wore a simple brown suit that had every button buttoned and every crease folded crisply. A starched white collar poked out from beneath the jacket, giving the Indian a quiet, respectful demeanor.

But it wasn't the Indian's suit that caught Clint's eye. Instead, it was the Indian's eyes, which seemed to flare up like embers when Clint looked directly into them. The glance couldn't have lasted more than a second, but it was a second that slowed down in Clint's mind until it almost ground to a halt.

And with a simple blink, it was over.

The hearing was still under way.

Jeremiah gave his story, which was quickly corroborated by the man who'd been tending bar that night at Kylie's. Despite the smug looks on the faces of the two injured gunmen, all of the evidence more or less fit together like a pair of gloves.

"What about you, Mr. Adams?" Judge Zellner asked. "Are you willing to tell your account?"

"Yes, sir," Clint said. From there, he launched into a simple retelling of what had happened. The events were so close to what had already been mentioned that if he hadn't been in a court of law, he might have just let the story stand as it was.

"I do have one thing to add, Your Honor," Clint said.

"Go ahead."

"Mr. Swann had just lost his daughter, and he wasn't exactly thinking straight. I've been in plenty of fights, so you might say I'm an expert in such things. It could have gone a lot worse than it did. If Jeremiah had wanted to kill anyone, he would have done it right away. I just thought it was necessary to step in before things went too far."

Judge Zellner let out a single grunt of a laugh. "Good job, Mr. Adams. Everything was pacified real nicely."

Before Clint could respond and before the stifled laughs in the courtroom could get too loud, Zellner held up his hand. "Sorry about that. That was out of line. The fact of the matter is that I've already acquitted Mr. Swann of his transgression. That's why he's sitting out there and not in a jail cell right now.

"As for you, Mr. Adams, I have no reason to doubt that you acted in the interest of self-defense as well as in the hopes of protecting Mr. Swann from himself as well as those two over there."

The wounded gunmen looked smug at first, which quickly shifted into confusion and then anger. As soon as they tried to stand up and defend themselves, they were roughly shoved back into their seats.

"I've already heard from you two," Zellner said to the gunmen. "Besides serving out your jail time, you'll also be responsible for paying for the damages done to Kylie's saloon. Now, let's move onto the second shooting incident which occurred down on Waylon Avenue."

THIRTY-FIVE

Once again, the judge sifted through some papers, looked them over and looked up again. "Mr. Adams, you and Miss Little were both mixed up in that. I've done a bit of research on my own and have come up with more than enough eyewitness accounts to form an opinion. Let's hear what you have to say about it."

Knowing better than to talk too much and hang himself in the process, Clint stuck to the facts about what had happened when he and Allison were attacked after coming out of the restaurant the day before. Judge Zellner nodded and took in the account without interruption and then did the same when Allison was given her chance to speak.

Thankfully, she took a cue from Clint and kept her story simple and to the point. That was followed by testimony from Dell, who'd been the only lawman at the scene. A few eyewitnesses stood up from the audience to verify a few things before sitting back down again.

All in all, it was quick and painless. One of the attackers who'd survived the incident spoke his piece and the other simply nodded to say that he agreed with his friend. Once that was over, the judge steepled his fingers and shrugged.

"Sounds cut and dried to me," Zellner said. "Unless

anyone else has something to say, I'm ready to make my decision." When nobody spoke up, Zellner grabbed his gavel and pronounced, "On both charges of murder, I find Clint Adams not guilty on grounds of self-defense. These two defendants from the Waylon Avenue shooting will also be serving jail time. The only thing saving you two from the noose is the fact that you didn't manage to kill anyone."

The lawyers appointed to speak for each side stood up and thanked the judge. Truth be told, Clint hadn't even realized the lawyers were there until that moment. The entire trial had been more of a direct exchange between the judge and those involved in the case. Considering how it had turned out, Clint couldn't really see much fault in that system.

"But make no mistake," Zellner added before Clint could feel too good about things. "This does not excuse your actions, Mr. Adams. For that account, it doesn't excuse yours either, Mr. Swann. We have law for a reason, and I do not take to vigilantes in my town."

Zellner fixed a steely glare onto Clint and Jeremiah before pounding his gavel once and making a sweeping gesture with his hand. "You men are dismissed. Miss Little, please step forward."

"What?" Allison and Clint both asked at the same time.

Sheriff Hayes had already stepped up behind Allison and put a hand on her shoulder. Although he wasn't forceful about it, there was no doubt that she wasn't going to be moving from that spot.

"She was right there with me yesterday," Clint explained. "We were both attacked. Some of the eyewitnesses even said so."

"All of the eyewitnesses said so," Judge Zellner clarified.

"Then why is there any question about her? I mean, if I was acting in self-defense, then she was, too. We were both jumped. We were both—"

Cutting Clint off with a swiftly upraised hand, Zellner

pounded his gavel against his desk with the other. "Mr. Adams, this other matter has nothing to do with you, and it has nothing to do with the incident from yesterday. Just because I ruled in your favor, don't think that I'll tolerate anything from you."

"What are the charges against her?" Clint asked.

"The charge is murder."

Clint glanced over to Allison. Although he felt surprised by what was happening, it wasn't something that hit him like a ton of bricks. He already knew she'd been hiding something, and he knew that she was more than capable of firing her gun. He even knew that she was plenty good at keeping a gun in arm's reach at any given time.

What interested Clint the most was the way she was reacting to the judge's words. She'd been protesting at first, but now her eyes were turned down and she slumped back into her chair. It was as if all the fight had been drained from her in a matter of seconds.

"The formal charge," Judge Zellner announced, "is the murder of Samuel Barkley which was perpetrated in Cheyenne, Wyoming. With the blessing of Cheyenne officials, the trial will be held here."

The judge had motioned toward another part of the courtroom where a group of unfamiliar lawmen were sitting. They nodded to acknowledge Zellner's words and shifted their eyes to Allison.

"Miss Little, how do you plead?"

Allison pulled in a breath and looked over to Clint. To him, more than to anyone else, she said, "Guilty."

THIRTY-SIX

Clint stayed for the duration of her hearing, but that didn't amount to much. Allison seemed uninterested in defending herself in the least after the charges were read. When she was accused of shooting a man in cold blood in the bed they'd shared, her response was only four words.

"It was self-defense."

Hearing that didn't do much to lessen the chill Clint was feeling when he recalled the gun he'd found under her pillow the night before. Even though he had enough confidence in his own reflexes to keep him from getting killed that way, he was starting to second-guess his decision to let that discovery slide by so quietly.

When it was all said and done, Zellner rapped his gavel against the top of his desk. "Since this case was dropped on me at the last minute," he said, once again looking over to the Cheyenne lawmen, "I'll take some time to review the evidence on my own. This court is adjourned until tomorrow. In the meantime, Sheriff Hayes will take Miss Little into custody. That will be all."

As much as he'd liked the lack of legal backtalk from the lawyers during his own trial, Clint now looked to the counselors with anger in his eyes. The subdued men in the fancy suits shook their heads and were already packing their papers up to call it a day.

Sheriff Hayes and his deputies were rounding up their prisoners after one of the men leaned over to remove the shackles from Clint's wrists. Even the prisoners themselves seemed content to let things lay where they were without saying anything more about it.

"Hold on here," Clint said over the ruckus of all the shuffling feet and murmuring voices. "Is that it?"

Zellner was up and headed for the door to his chambers. "What else is there, Mr. Adams?"

"I'm let go and Allison is jailed without a full trial?"

"I had time to look into your case, Mr. Adams. I'll take that same amount of time to look into hers. Unless you want to join her in a cell for contempt, I suggest you let it go at that and show up tomorrow morning to see how it turns out."

With that said, Zellner tossed a wave over his shoulder and disappeared through the narrow door leading out of the courtroom. The door shut behind him with as much finality as the gavel slamming against the hardwood tabletop.

Clint looked around and found that all the people who'd been surrounding him before were now making their way out of the courthouse. The sight of one man in particular got him rushing in that direction himself.

The Indian he'd spotted was just leaving. As the man passed one of the deputies, he was stopped by a quick, rough hand.

"Hold on there," Chapman said. He'd been the one to reach out and grab the Indian, even as he kept hold of one of the wounded prisoners with his other hand. "Just what the hell do you think you were doing in there?"

The Indian blinked in confusion. That confusion turned to fear as he was quickly surrounded by armed lawmen.

"What's going on here?" Sheriff Hayes asked.

"This one here was taking a hell of an interest in this trial," Chapman said.

"So did a lot of other folks. What's your point?"

"He's an Indian. We're looking for an Indian." He turned to one of the others who'd been at the trial. This was a man brought along to lend his testimony of what he'd seen in the second of Clint's fights. "Tell him, Ernie," Chapman said, turning to look at another member of the audience. "Tell him we're looking for an Indian."

"Sure enough," Ernie Niedelander said.

"So because he's got red skin, you want to string him up?" After the sheriff asked that question, he didn't much like what he saw written on his deputies' faces. "Get out of here," Hayes said to the Indian. "Same for you, Adams. I won't have you interfering in my duties."

"I don't intend on interfering, Sheriff. I want to help."

"I don't need your help. You can pick up your gun at my office once I get these prisoners squared away. Other than that, we've got no business."

"What about Jeremiah's daughter?" Clint asked. "What about Allison's sister? They might have been killed by the same man." Jogging to get in front of the group of lawmen, Clint added, "It could have been the same man who killed your deputy."

That stopped Hayes sure enough. The sheriff pushed Allison into the arms of another of his men before walking up to stand toe-to-toe with Clint. "We don't know for certain who killed my deputy. The only reason you or your woman here are not on my list is because so many others at your hotel heard you two carrying on like a couple of newlyweds.

"So if I were you, I'd take the judge's advice and let sleeping dogs lie. I'm taking care of this killer and will bring him in my own way." The more Sheriff Hayes talked, the more venom he put into his words. Finally, he seemed to be spitting them out like steam from a piston. "That murdering bastard will die for what he's done, and I'll bring his carcass into town for everyone to see. That should make Jeremiah and Miss Little here real happy."

Clint took in what was being said, although he was actually studying the faces around him the most. The lawmen were behind their sheriff every step of the way. They were also mad as hell and chomping at the bit to spill some blood themselves.

"You still plan on taking that man in?" Clint asked Chapman.

The deputy still had a firm grip on the Indian's shoulder. In fact, that grip seemed to be getting tighter by the second as his knuckles whitened around the clump of jacket he'd grabbed.

"Never you mind, Adams," Chapman warned.

"I thought the law in this town didn't look kindly toward vigilantes."

"Adams is right," Sheriff Hayes said. "I said let that man go and I meant it."

"He's coming with us," Chapman said. "After all that's happened, we got just cause to hold this redskin until we learn he ain't who we're after."

Hayes let out a flustered sigh and shot a fiery glare at his deputy. Before he argued his point any further, he took a look at the crowd that was starting to gather around him and his men. The sheriff choked back what he wanted to say and instead pushed his own prisoner forward.

Chapman followed without another word with his prisoner.

The Indian looked to Clint silently, but there wasn't anything for Clint to do at that point except watch.

In moments, he felt someone move up and stand beside him.

"You think that's the man?" Jeremiah asked from Clint's side.

Clint shook his head. "I don't know. Seems to me like this whole thing is just too wild to be tamed. Just when I think the reins can be pulled in, it all bucks in another direction."

"Maybe that's because you haven't seen all there is to see."

"Or it could be that I'm in over my head," Clint offered. "Either that or I just don't know what the hell I'm doing."

The blacksmith's thick, callused hand settled on Clint's shoulder. "I think you and me are the only ones with our eyes open in this town. The rest of the folks just don't want to look at it all 'cause it's so damn ugly."

Clint turned to look at the blacksmith. The first time he'd met Jeremiah, the other man's eyes had been wild and unfocused. Now they were eerily calm. They were the same eyes seen in photographs of soldiers on fresh battle-fields. They were eyes that had seen more than they'd ever wanted to see.

At that moment, Clint felt like he was looking into a mirror.

THIRTY-SEVEN

The closer Jeremiah got to the stump outside of town where his little girl had been found, the colder and more distant he became. By the time they got close enough to see the black stains on the bark, Jeremiah was practically a walking corpse.

With a great deal of effort, he tore his eyes from the stump and looked down at the ground near his feet. He pointed and knelt down, motioning for Clint to do the same.

"Right here," Jeremiah said. "You see it?"

Clint saw it all right. The carving on the root was plain as day. "Is this what the law was looking at before?"

Jeremiah nodded. "They had Ernie Niedelander take a look at it since he's the only one around here who might know what it means."

"Why would he know? Does he study Indian languages?"

"I guess. All I know is that he used to serve in the cavalry out in Cherokee territory."

"Really? Do you know what unit?"

Jeremiah thought about that for a moment, but wound up shaking his head. "Don't know for certain. Come to

146

think of it, I'm not even sure many folks know about his cavalry days."

"Why's that?"

"Because Ernie don't like to talk much about it. Can't say as I blame him considering how bad I heard it got out there. Some of the stories I heard would curl your toes."

"You might be surprised."

Clint didn't have to imagine what kind of stories Jeremiah was talking about. He'd heard plenty of them and had witnessed plenty for himself. He'd seen enough blood spilled on both sides of the feud between the Indians and the Army to last a lifetime.

Clint had also known plenty of soldiers in his lifetime. They were a mixed lot, but the changes they went through followed a fairly stable pattern. Normally, they went into uniform full of piss and vinegar. The more time they spent wearing their colors, however, the quieter they got, until they wound up with the cold, haunted eyes from all those photographs.

"So do you talk to this Niedelander fellow a lot?" Clint asked.

"Not particularly."

"Then how do you know so much about him?"

Jeremiah shrugged. "I shoed his horse a few times. Once when he first came into town and again a little while after that. You can learn a lot about a man by taking a look at the horse he rides."

"I bet. And what did you learn about him?"

"First off, Ernie's horse wasn't a fancy breed, but it was a hell of a runner. It was the kind of animal that gets picked out by a man with a real good eye for horses. That horse was taken care of real good, too. I even spotted a few spots where the shoes had been fixed on the spot. The work was rough, but it was sturdy as hell and did the job real nice."

"So you think he's had training?" Clint asked.

"Military training was my guess. The patches I saw there were like some others I seen from an old cavalry man's horse. Those boys know how to tend to their animals."

"They should. Their lives depend on it."

"You got that right. Plus, there was a few little things here and there I saw, like the way straps were tucked into buckles or the way he tied off his reins. Even the way he climbed down from the saddle and the boots he wore told me something. Guess that's what I get for shoeing so many horses and talking with so many riders."

"So you asked him about riding in the cavalry?"

"Sure did. Just making conversation, you know. He was a bit surprised, but not overly such." Jeremiah cocked his head and looked down at Clint. "This have anything to do with them markings?"

"No. Just making conversation."

"So what do you think them markings are?"

"I've seen something like them once or twice. I've also seen enough Indian markings to know that this isn't one of them. Well, not completely."

"Huh?"

"Let's just say they're a real good copy, but not quite the genuine article."

"So that was just made to look like an Indian did it?"

Clint nodded. "Probably by someone who'd spent a lot of time with them. Indian marks aren't just slapped on any old thing."

"Well, whoever did this can't be in their right mind."

"True. But if they took the time to carve this in after dropping off your little girl, it's a wonder they weren't spotted, isn't it?"

Jeremiah straightened up. He looked around for a moment and then nodded. "Yeah. It sure as hell is."

"That is, unless they were familiar enough to folks around here that they wouldn't get a second glance from people passing by." Clint stood up and dusted himself off.

"There's a few Indians around here, but they're not exactly a common sight in Claymore, are they?"

"No," Jeremiah replied solemnly. "They sure as hell ain't."

THIRTY-EIGHT

The sky was a dark purple when Clint made his way back to Sheriff Hayes's office. As far as sheriff's offices went, the place was fairly standard. Desks in the front of the room and cells in the back. By the looks of it, this office doubled as a jailhouse, because there were close to a dozen cells in there separated from the front by half of a wall.

When Clint stepped into the office, he was surprised at how quiet it was. That was downright strange considering that more than half the cells were full and there was even a lady in one of them that most of those men couldn't normally have gotten close to unless they were paying her or chained to her ankle.

"How're you holding up?" Clint asked.

Allison was laying on the cot in her cell. She only moved enough to look up at him and then shrug. "Good as can be expected, I suppose."

"Is it true?"

"Is what true?"

"What the judge said about you," Clint said. "About what you did. Is it true?"

"The son of a bitch I killed is better off dead. At least,"

she added while bowing her head again and closing her eyes, "the rest of us are better off without him."

There was something in her eyes that seemed vaguely familiar. It was a pain that Clint had seen on the faces of other women he'd known. "What did he do to you? Did he rape you?"

That question worked for Clint in two ways. First of all, it cut through everything else and saved a bit of time. Also, it woke her up quicker than a cold slap across her face.

"Rape me?" she said, swinging her legs over the side of her cot. "Not hardly. I doubt the asshole could've managed it. Hell, he barely managed it anyway."

"Then why kill him?"

"Yeah," Sheriff Hayes said as he stepped up next to Clint with his arms folded across his chest. "I'd like to hear that one myself."

Allison didn't bat an eye at the sudden appearance of the sheriff. She didn't even pause before saying, "I killed him because he was real good friends with the scum that killed my sister. He liked to kill women and he meant to kill me. I just beat him to the punch."

"Can you be sure about that?" Hayes asked.

"He's done it before," Allison said. "Only he killed whores and Chinese. You know, the kind of women that don't get the full protection of men in badges like yourself."

Hayes didn't have anything to say in response to that. Although he looked as though he simply didn't want to dignify the accusation with a response, his eyes said something different. Clint could see it just below the surface.

The sheriff's eyes had a bit of anger in there, mixed with a touch of shame.

"So how do you know you didn't kill the man who killed your sister?" Clint asked.

"Because that one kills women," Allison replied. "The

man I'm after kills girls. He doesn't like it any other way. I heard it from someone who knows."

"And you're sure that wasn't a lie you heard?"

"It wasn't a lie. I know that for damn sure. The fact that other girls have died the same way proves that well enough."

"We'll hear all this tomorrow in front of Judge Zellner," Hayes said. "If you wanted to speak to the prisoner, you should have asked me first, Adams."

"I'd appreciate another moment to talk to Allison, if that's all right."

Hayes looked between them and nodded. "Five minutes. After that, I'm tossing you out of here and that's final." Without waiting for another word to be said, Hayes turned on his heels and walked back to his desk. Once there, he propped up his feet and pulled a watch from his pocket.

"That asshole will time his two minutes right down to the last second," Allison snipped.

"Then let's not waste a moment here," Clint replied. "You went after more than the one man you killed. I know that for certain."

"So what if I did? They was killers, every last one of them. They got what they deserved and then some."

"I'd like to believe you, but you weren't exactly up front with me, were you?"

"And would you have been just fine and dandy if I'd told you what I was after? Would you have understood if I'd told you the things I've done?"

"That doesn't matter anymore. What does matter is that those things you did don't go to waste."

Allison's eyes narrowed as she got closer to the bars of her cell. "What do you mean?"

"You found some other killers who know the man you're after. They know the man we're both after."

She nodded.

"You found them and you killed them, but not before you got something from them. Am I right?"

Her nod was subtle this time, but was there all the same.

"How many of them were there?"

After a deep breath, Allison said, "Three."

"And what about the gun under your pillow last night?" Clint asked, focusing on her eyes. "Was that meant for me if I stepped out of line?"

Allison paused, but it was more of a guilty reaction to getting caught than anything else. "That's a habit," she said. "Nothing more."

Clint didn't have to study her too hard to know that she was telling the truth. The fact of the matter was that he hadn't really felt threatened by her even when he did find that gun. After what he knew about her and what had happened, he couldn't exactly fault her for being cautious.

"You have to answer for what you did," Clint told her. "But I'll stand up for you in court to see that you don't get anything more."

She smiled and reached a hand out through the bars which Clint immediately took hold of. "Actually, I'm not too worried about that," Allison said. "I think this judge may actually be one of the good ones."

"Yeah. And even though you're in here, that doesn't mean the man who killed these girls will go free. I intend on putting a stop to him before he gets his hands on anyone else."

"Don't promise that, Clint. He could be killing someone else's sister right now."

As much as Clint wanted to refute that, he couldn't. Some comforting words came to mind, but he knew they wouldn't help Allison much at all. So rather than try to comfort her, he went on with the job he'd taken. "Were there markings by the spot where your sister was found?"

"Yes. There were markings by all the others, too. At least, the ones I know of."

"What did they look like?"

Allison shrugged and shook her head. "Like something in some Indian drawing, I guess."

"Can you draw them for me?"

A haunted look came over her face as she nodded. "Yes."

"Do it."

She went to the wall of her cell that was next to the bars, bent down and picked up a small pebble that had come in off of someone's boot. Using that pebble, she scratched a few designs onto the wall, scraping away dirt and dust rather than scratching too far into the wall itself.

When she was finished, she stepped back so Clint could see the designs she'd made.

Clint looked at them for a few moments as footsteps came up from behind him.

"Time's up," Sheriff Hayes said. "Hey! Did you scratch up my wall?"

The pictures weren't detailed, but neither was the carving that had been found on the root. Clint looked back and forth between each of them, every so often shifting his head to one side so he could see them from different angles.

"Are you sure these are the markings?" he asked Allison.

She nodded without hesitation. "I see them in my dreams."

A smile formed on Clint's face. "Thank you. This is more help than you know."

"I said time's up," Hayes announced. "Come collect your pistol and be on your way."

Clint allowed himself to be escorted away from the cells and to the sheriff's desk. Once there, he was handed his modified Colt while another deputy opened the door and held it. Clint walked for the door while almost dropping his gun after trying to slide it into a holster he wasn't wearing.

It was a habit. Nothing more.

THIRTY-NINE

"What are you doing out here?"

After he'd asked that question, Dell waited and saw that he might as well have spoken to a brick wall.

Clint was on one knee hunching over the root which had become such a focal point in the last few days. He had a burning match in his hand to cast a flickering light over no more than an inch or two of ground. There wasn't much wind blowing, but it seemed cold enough to snuff the match out on its own.

Dell stepped forward with his hands stuffed into his pockets. "Adams? What are you doing out here?"

When Clint stood up, the wind was able to get a cleaner shot at the match in his hand. That was enough to put out the flame before he flicked the burnt stick to the dirt.

"Just getting another look at this marking."

"Someone already got a look at it," Dell said. "He told me it's definitely Indian." His eyes drifted toward the stump. One of the deputies had chopped away the blood-stained bark just so they could put the grisly memories out of everyone's mind, but it wasn't enough. "Damn savages."

"Did you get a chance to talk to Allison about the marks she saw?"

155

"No, but I heard you two talking about them back at the sheriff's office."

"Did you get a look at the drawings she did?"

Dell nodded. "Looked like chicken scratch to me."

"Well, it did to me as well." Clint dug in his pocket and pulled out a folded piece of paper. He unfolded it and showed it to the deputy. "That's them as near as I can recall. What do you think?"

The deputy looked over the paper as well as the markings Clint had made on them, which resembled the scratches on the jail wall. "That's them, more or less. You want me to have Ernie take a look at them? He knows what he's talking about when it comes to these Injuns."

"No need for that. Just take another look at them."

Glancing back and forth between Clint's face and the paper in his hand, Dell rubbed his own hands together before taking the paper Clint had offered. Clint had removed another match from his pocket and was reaching down for something on the ground nearby.

"Why didn't you use that before?" Dell asked when he saw the lantern Clint was lighting.

"Because I didn't want to draw too much attention to myself. Now that you're here and we're having this conversation, I'd say a lantern doesn't make much difference anymore."

Once the wick was lit, Clint turned the lantern's knob until a soft glow came from within the curved glass. Although the markings on the paper were easier to see, they still didn't make any more sense than before.

"Take a look at the second one," Clint said, pointing to the least complicated of the marks.

Dell studied it for a few seconds and nodded.

"Now," Clint said while taking the paper back and turning it on its side, "take a look at the first one."

At first, Dell didn't see anything. Then, it hit him. "They look similar, only one's got a few more details."

"Now look at the third one," Clint said. Once again, he took hold of the paper and turned it, so that it was upside down from where it had started.

"It looks kind of like the other two, except . . . more."

"Kind of like different stages of the same picture," Clint said.

The confusion on Dell's face cleared up when he heard that. He snapped his fingers and looked over to Clint. "That's right! Almost like someone was showing someone else how to put together one picture by splitting it up into a bunch of steps."

"Now look at that root," Clint said while lowering himself and the lantern down to ground level.

After a bit of squinting and cocking his head from one side to another, Dell smiled broadly. "I'll be damned."

"You see it?"

"I sure do. If I look at it, I can see every one of those other marks in that one. There's only a few lines added."

"Unfortunately, I have a bad notion of what those lines mean."

"What do they mean?"

"I don't think these are Indian markings at all, although it's plain to see that whoever drew them wants them to look that way." Pausing for a moment, Clint asked, "Have you ever seen the handle of a killer's gun?"

Although Dell's eyes snapped to the Colt now holstered around Clint's waist, he didn't say the first words that came to his mind. Instead, he thought again and nodded. "We've brought in a few gunfighters. Not many, but I did get a look at their guns."

"Some of the up-and-coming bad men like to mark their kills with notches on their guns. If you read too many yellowback novels, you'd think they all did that."

Dell smirked guiltily. "Yeah, you would."

"We already know the killer we're after takes pride in his work. I think he also gets a thrill out of rubbing what he does into the faces of everyone who tries to come after him. He's not stupid enough to make it easy for the law to catch him, but he's cocky enough to mark his kills right where everyone can see it."

"So these really are steps building into the same picture," Dell pointed out.

Clint nodded. "He's finishing the picture one notch at a time, counting off each drop of innocent blood he spills. I even saw a notch in the handle of the rifle used to kill that man right in front of both of us not too long ago."

"So you don't think he'll stop until he gets done with his picture?"

Shaking his head, Clint replied, "There's too many notches in these pictures already, but it'll probably never be enough for him. He's not going to stop on his own. Not until someone comes along who can stop him."

Dell's features had become cold as the wind. Nodding solemnly, he asked, "What can I do to help?"

FORTY

They were getting too close.

At first, when the killer had been keeping watch on them, seeing the law and then Clint Adams stumble like blind men was entertaining. The entertainment stopped, however, once the blindness started to lift and their stumbling began taking on a purpose of its own.

Not all of the men coming after him were so blind.

And they were no longer stumbling.

Laying with his belly flat against the cold, hard-packed earth, the killer focused his eyes on the two figures near the stump outside of town. He'd started off simply following Dell to see where the deputy might be going, but that had led him to where Clint Adams was lurking in the shadows.

The killer cursed under his breath. Although he didn't make a sound, the profanity leaked from his mouth as a wisp of steam from between clenched teeth.

If he'd had his rifle with him, the killer might have taken a shot right then and there. He knew he could pick off Adams just as easily as picking a bottle off a fence post. His target was right out in the open, pretty as you please, begging for someone to put him out of his misery.

Out of the killer's misery was more like it.

The law, Clint Adams, even Allison Little had been so close outside of the courthouse but they hadn't even realized it. They'd been so close to him and they'd let him go.

Maybe even a few of them had their suspicions, but that was doubtful. Thinking about that made the killer shake his head. The law didn't know anything more than when they'd started. They were still chasing their own tails like good little doggies.

Clint Adams and Allison Little were different, though.

Clint wasn't chasing anything. He was hunting.

As for Allison, she always kept close enough for the killer to be able to see her when he wanted. She was dangerous, to be sure, but handling her had never been much of a problem. That is, until recently.

Allison was a thorn in the killer's side, mainly because she drifted closer and closer to him every day. Since the killer hadn't wanted to be rid of her just yet, the fact that she'd landed in jail was a blessing in disguise.

That just left Clint Adams and that deputy. By the looks of it, both of them were going to present a problem which would need to be dealt with very soon.

With that firmly in mind, the killer shifted his eyes away from Adams and the deputy to another, more comforting sight. It was a sight that reminded him of a sunrise. Although he'd seen it plenty of times, it was always breathtaking. And every time he saw it, the beauty was just a little bit different.

It took a moment for the killer's eyes to adjust to the difference in light since he was now looking at something illuminated by a few different lanterns. The window he found himself gazing into was of average size, but seemed to get larger the more he stared.

The light coming from behind that glass was warm and comforting to him. It made him forget about all the trouble that was working its way closer to him by the second. When he got a look at the little girl he knew to be inside that house, the killer actually sucked in a quick breath.

His eyes started to water at the sight of her shiny gold hair and the soft, innocent curve of her cheeks. Without thinking about it, he'd walked up closer to that window so he could get a better look inside. His instincts also told him when to stop, before he got close enough to be spotted by a casual eye.

As much as he wanted to walk up and place his hands flat on the glass, he stopped himself from doing so. As much as he wanted to knock on that door and walk inside, he stopped himself. As much as he wanted to slide his fingers through that golden hair and then slice it off of her head, he stopped himself.

Well, maybe held himself back was more accurate.

He would do all of those things soon enough. He just needed to wait until he'd dealt with the stupid men who wanted to put him behind bars.

And once he'd taken those men out of the picture, everything that came after would be so much sweeter.

The killer smiled to himself, stuck his hands deep into his pockets and walked away. He passed someone on the street who simply looked over and nodded to him.

They were all so stupid.

FORTY-ONE

Dell's knuckles cracked against the worn wood of the door frame. The sound of it echoed through the small house almost as much as it echoed down the nearly deserted street.

"Ernie?" the deputy said to the door. "You in there?"

He knocked again.

"Wake up, Ernie, it's Dell. The sheriff wants to ask you some questions."

The deputy stood in the cold shadows for another few moments without getting any results from the noise he'd been making. He knocked a few more times while shaking his head, knowing that he probably wasn't going to get anything from that attempt either.

The house wasn't very big. Apart from the door frame, there was a single, rectangular window on the front wall. Even though there was no light coming from behind the linen curtains drawn over the window, Dell leaned over to peer through the glass anyway.

Although there wasn't anything moving inside the house as far as he could see, Dell's hand inched toward the gun at his side. More and more, he was thinking that he should have taken the time to let the sheriff know what he planned to do.

But there wasn't much time left. Every second that ticked by was another second the killer in their midst was allowed to roam free. Now that he had a notion of what needed to be done, Dell couldn't find it in himself to put it off any longer.

To much innocent blood had been spilled already. Probably more than he would even care to know.

"Come on, Ernie," Dell said as he rapped on the door frame while squinting into the corner of the window. "Wake up and come on out. It's important."

Suddenly there was some movement inside.

Dell couldn't be certain, but he thought he saw someone crouching in the darkness and moving from one side of the room to the other. His hand pressed against the grip of his pistol as his fingers tightened around the handle. One finger slipped under the trigger guard as he started to bring the gun up from its holster.

"Ernie?"

The movement had stopped. Either that, or whoever was moving had gotten into a shadow that was dark enough to conceal him completely. With his eyes focused so intently on the spot where he'd last seen that motion, Dell practically jumped out of his skin when a figure reared up directly in front of him.

"Holy . . . !" Dell started to shout. He stopped himself when he got a look at the face looking back at him from the other side of the window. It was Clint.

Smirking a bit at the fright he'd given the deputy, Clint nodded once toward the front door and then moved off in that direction. A few seconds later, the handle moved and the front door swung open. Dell was still clutching his chest as he walked inside.

"You knew I was heading around back of the place, right?" Clint said while closing the door behind the deputy.

Dell stood inside the little house, doing his best to disguise the fact that his heart was still pounding against his ribs. "Yeah, I knew. I just didn't know that you were going to get inside."

"It didn't take much work," Clint said with a shrug. The fact of the matter was close to what he'd said, but not quite. It had been a relatively easy task to get the back door open. Easy, that is, for someone who'd watched a few talented robbers at work.

"I don't think we should be in here," Dell said warily.

Clint was already looking around the place. Once he'd found a lantern and turned the knob so the slightest of glows came from its wick, he said, "If Ernie comes in, just tell him you caught me inside here. I'll say I got the wrong house and we can take it from there."

"That still won't make my job any easier in explaining this to Sheriff Hayes."

"What about if we found something in here to let us know that we were on the right track?"

Dell nodded while still glancing nervously out the window. "That would make things a lot easier."

"Then you can relax. I think we just hit paydirt."

FORTY-TWO

Although Clint knew better than to doubt himself when his instincts were screaming at him from every angle, there was always that little voice in the back of his head letting him know that he might be wrong. That little voice was silenced when he found and opened the flat, dented box underneath the rickety bed in the modest little house.

"Where did you say Ernie Niedelander is from?" Clint asked as he pulled the box out from where it had been stashed.

"I know he served in the cavalry in a few places, but I'm pretty sure he spent some time in Cheyenne."

"And how long has he lived here?"

"A few months, maybe. What did you find?"

Clint leaned to one side so Dell could finally get a look at what had captured so much of his attention. The box was open to reveal a stack of neatly folded cloth.

Dell looked down at the cloth and then back to Clint. "What the hell is that supposed to be?"

Delicately, reverently, Clint took hold of the top piece of cloth between thumbs and forefingers. He lifted it to show that it wasn't just cloth, but a plain white slip. There

165

wasn't much fancy about the slip, and it was small enough to be mistaken for a large napkin or even a rag.

It was just big enough to fit a little girl.

"Does Ernie have anyone this might belong to?" Clint asked.

Dell shook his head. "No," he said, reflexively backing away from the sight of the slip. "He doesn't."

Clint turned the slip over and found something on the bottom hem. After taking a closer look, he held it up for Dell to see. "Does that look familiar?"

Grimacing as though he was leaning closer to a dead body, the deputy forced himself to take another look at the slip. By doing that alone, he could see the slip had been worn. There was dirt smudged into the material as well as something darker that Clint was showing him.

That darker spot looked like a stain at first. Then, it was plain to see that it was no stain. It was a marking smeared in a dark, crusted substance. Dell's eyes narrowed after studying the mark for less than a second. It was more or less exactly like one of the markings scratched onto the jail wall.

"Is that blood?" Dell asked.

Although Clint was fairly certain, he needed to be sure. He steeled himself and took a quick, closer look. Once he'd gotten what he was after, he dropped the slip and stood up.

"Yeah," Clint said as the rage started to build inside of him. "It's blood."

"How many are in there?"

Clint tapped the box with his foot just hard enough to rustle its contents. "Looks like at least six or seven. Maybe more."

The fact of the matter was that Clint had seen enough. He'd gotten closer than he'd ever wanted to get to one of the most chilling things he'd ever discovered. Once the re-alization sunk in about what each of those little girls' slips represented, he was left with a cold, seething anger in his belly.

"Jesus Christ," Dell said while looking around at the house. "It's really him, isn't it? Ernie's the one that killed little Mary Swann."

"Yeah," Clint said, unable to take his eyes away from the box at his feet. "Plus God only knows how many more."

"How could we have missed him? How'd you know it was him?"

"I didn't until tonight. What I knew for certain was that the killer was probably still in town. An animal like that would get a kick out of seeing all the misery he's caused. After talking to Allison about what happened to her and how close it was to what happened here, I guessed that the signs pointing to an Indian as the killer were just there to throw people off the track."

Dell averted his eyes when he heard that, knowing that he'd been one of those most thrown off-track by what Ernie had told him.

"When that man was shot right in front of me, after Allison and I were attacked," Clint said, "we looked to see if we could find him. We were lucky enough to find the rifle which I'd bet anything I have was the one used to do that shooting."

"How come you didn't bring any of this to the sheriff?" Dell asked.

"Because all of you were off on your own hunt, and I didn't have any reason to get in your way. I took that rifle apart and didn't find much of anything apart from a notch in the handle. It's not a lot, but it says something to someone who knows how gunmen think.

"I also found the gun to be cleaner than new. It was maintained in a way that usually goes along with a man in the military."

When he saw the impression he was leaving on the

deputy, Clint added, "Just another hunch. I do a lot of work with guns."

That didn't do anything to dampen the admiration in Dell's expression. "So you figure whoever shot that man was in the military?"

"Either that," Clint said, "or he was using a gun belonging to someone in the military. Of course, a gun that well tended is usually pretty hard to get away from its owner. It's kind of like forgetting to bring your right hand along with you when you head out for the day. It just doesn't happen."

Clint set the lid back onto the box and pushed it under the bed. He did so more to get it out of his sight than to tidy up. "What was done to that little girl, and all the others as far as I've heard, doesn't point so much to an Indian as someone who knows a lot about them and who even has a dislike for them. Actually, hatred would be more fitting."

Dell's face twisted into a doubtful expression as he reluctantly started to shake his head. "I never heard Ernie say anything about hating Indians."

"He was in the cavalry?"

"Yes."

"Then he's had some dealings with Indians. More than likely, they weren't very good. Although not all cavalry officers hate the Indians, that's usually a fairly good assumption. At the very least, you can bet he knows a lot about them."

"He sure does know a lot about Indians. That's why we asked him to have a look at that mark we found."

"And he was more than willing to look, wasn't he?"

"Yeah," Dell replied. "Ernie was willing to help."

"You know how scalping got started?"

Dell blinked and said, "Indians."

Clint shook his head. "Indian hunters scalped the ones they killed. It was less for them to carry when they went in to claim their pay for the blood they spilled. The Indians that do scalp are doing it for the same reasons, and most of them were taught to do it by the military men looking to clear out their territories of the tribes."

"That's not what I heard."

"There's plenty of accounts, but that one's true enough. If a man can get himself to kill a little girl, he probably looks at scalping as just another messy chore. I've only met a few who think that way about skinning another human being, and they had an awful lot in common with Ernie Niedelander."

Clint could see the shadow coming over Dell's face. It wasn't so much that he was doubting what he heard. It was more like he couldn't find a way to push down the dread that came from hearing it.

"Tell me something," Clint said. "When you took Ernie to that marking, did you have to point it out to him?"

Pausing for a moment, Dell thought that over. He eventually shook his head. "Not as such. He met me there."

"Kind of like he already knew where it was?"

Dell didn't respond to that. He was in the middle of sorting through every last word that had passed between him and Ernie Niedelander.

"Look," Clint said. "There was plenty that led me to this man. He's got the knowledge needed to lay a trail convincing enough to send the law on a chase to find some imaginary Indian. He's got the background that fits the gun I found, and he just happened to be in the right place at the right time to steer everyone right where he needed them to go.

"I know getting in here like this doesn't set too well with you, but all you need to do is look in that box under that bed to know we found the right man. Why not take advantage of what we found? As long as it puts a stop to these killings, what's the difference?"

"The difference is acting like a lawman and acting like a vigilante."

"Then there's something else I should tell you that might make you feel a whole lot better."

Dell perked up a bit and nodded. When Clint told him about the trump card he'd been saving, the deputy smirked. That smirk lasted right up until Clint's eyes jerked toward the back door and he swiveled on the balls of his feet to face in that direction.

"I sincerely wish you hadn't come in here like this," Ernie Niedelander said.

FORTY-THREE

The man didn't look like anyone Clint or even Dell recognized. It was as if the eyes of a predator were now staring out through a once-familiar face. Where before he seemed like a reserved, almost cowed man, he now looked more like a lean animal crouching in preparation for an attack.

His head was turned down a bit, and his eyes glared up at both men with a cold intensity.

"What are you men doing in my house?" Ernie asked.

While Dell was more concerned with smoothing over what he saw as a transgression, Clint was more focused on the rifle in Ernie's hand.

"I can explain this, Ernie," Dell said as he stepped forward with both hands in front of him.

Clint reached out to grab hold of the deputy's elbow before he could get any farther. Dell tried to pull himself free at first, but quickly saw the reason why Clint was being so cautious.

"There's no need for the gun, Ernie," Dell said. "Why don't you hand that over and we can explain ourselves?"

Ernie didn't budge. Although he was more or less shrouded in darkness, Clint could still make out the delib-

171

erate shifting of the man's eyes as he took in his home and the two uninvited guests now standing in it.

"A man's got the right to defend his house," Ernie said. "And there isn't a lawful reason for you to be in here."

"What about the box under your bed?" Clint asked, sensing the deputy was becoming more flustered by the second. "I suppose you can explain that away?"

"You mean my daughter's clothes? She died when she was little and I kept a few of her things to remember her by. Is there a law against a man being sentimental?"

"No. But there's a law against a man being a murderer."

Ernie blinked once and took a breath. The fact that he didn't move at all besides that was disconcerting even for Clint.

Although the man's presence was chilling, Clint used that to steel himself as he subtly moved Dell aside and squared his shoulders up with Niedelander. "There's some kind of markings on those clothes," Clint said. "They match marks found close to the bodies of other little girls. Little dead girls."

Every move Clint made and word he said was a way to test Niedelander. He read the smaller man the way he would read an opponent at a high-stakes poker game. Considering just how high the stakes were this time around, it didn't seem like too far of a stretch.

Niedelander took a moment, as though he was studying Clint and Dell the same way he was being studied. Shifting his gaze toward Clint, it seemed as though he'd suddenly decided that Dell no longer existed. "I tried to help find the one that killed the Swann girl."

Clint kept his eyes fixed on Niedelander. He knew that faltering in the slightest right about now would be like baring his neck to a rabid dog. "You were helping to steer the law in the wrong direction. Just like you tried to cover your tracks when you shot that man who was about to tell me all about how you sparked that fight outside that restaurant."

Cocking his head to one side, Clint said, "In fact, he did tell me a little about someone he saw talking to Pete back then. Someone told Pete just enough bullshit to get him riled up and headed in my direction. Come to think of it, you fit that description pretty well."

Niedelander flinched at that one. The muscles in his jaw tensed like he was clamping down on something he meant to tear into pieces.

"You came here to arrest me?" Niedelander asked.

"We came here to follow up on a few things," Clint replied. "But I think the sheriff won't mind having a talk with you. Isn't that right, Dell?"

The deputy looked back and forth between the two men. "Yeah. Put that gun down and come along with me, Ernie."

"This is a mistake," Niedelander said.

"If that's so, then it's best to get it out of the way so we can move on."

"You've got the wrong man."

"What did it feel like to kill those girls?" Clint asked.

The sudden shift in the conversation struck a nerve since it had been snuck in like a well-timed jab. Niedelander was glancing back and forth between Dell and Clint, unsure as to what face he should put on. Hearing the bluntness of Clint's question forced him to pull in a quick breath and tighten his grip around the rifle in his hand.

Clint took half a step forward, making sure to keep his eyes firmly locked upon Niedelander. "Did it feel anything like hunting down those Indians back when you had nobody to answer to and a uniform to justify your actions?"

Another twitch from Niedelander told Clint that he'd snuck in another jab.

"The men I killed were filthy savages," Niedelander snarled, baring his teeth and letting a string of spit hang down from the corner of his mouth. "They were killers and devils, all of them!"

"So that made you a hero?" Clint asked. "Or did it just

give you a taste for blood? I think maybe it started as one and turned into the other."

"You don't know a goddamn thing, Adams!"

"Ernie, calm down," Dell said as he stepped up to put one arm across Clint's chest to hold him back. "Put that gun down and say whatever you need to say."

But Niedelander didn't pay any mind to the deputy. He was wringing his hands around the rifle while slowly bringing it up to a firing position. "We had a job to do and we did it. I was a decorated cavalry officer!"

"When did you start killing girls?" Clint asked.

Before he could stop himself, Niedelander blurted out, "The first one was an accident." He blinked as he realized what he'd said. When he looked back to Clint, there was a bit of relief in his eyes. The reserved face he'd put on for the deputy was gone completely now. "It was an accident, but it felt so good. And it'll feel just as good when I kill the both of you."

FORTY-FOUR

Dell had another plea on the tip of his tongue when Niedelander brought up his rifle. Luckily for him, Clint was no longer in the mood for conversation and shoved Dell aside with a quickly outstretched arm. Although the hit was painful, it was enough to get the deputy out of the way in time for Clint to do the same.

Niedelander wasn't smiling as he brought up the rifle. Unlike many other gunmen, it wasn't the shooting that sent the tingle through his skin. He wouldn't be smiling until he got his first sight of blood. By the expectant look on his face, he was counting down the seconds before that happened.

Once he saw that Dell was toppling over to one side, Clint threw himself in the other. In his head, the moments were dragging by with lead feet. Finally, Niedelander pulled his trigger and the little house filled with equal parts fire and thunder.

The thunder came from the rifle's breech as well as the chamber itself. The fire came from the barrel, but not as much as one might have expected. Instead, most of the sparks were directed up from the spot where the barrel met with the chambered round. A flash came from the end of the barrel, while triple the amount of fury was directed back up into Niedelander's face.

Niedelander let out a shrieking cry that made him seem even more like an animal. He pitched the rifle to the floor, but the damage had already been done. The flesh on his hands, arms, face and neck was blistered and peeling back in strips. The spots around his wounds were already beet red or blackened by the blast. Here and there, shards of copper were wedged into his skin.

Dell looked down to see if he'd been hit. He then looked over to see if Clint had taken the bullet. Still coming up empty, he glanced around in confusion as if he could see where the hell the rifle's bullet had gone.

"Remember that last shred of proof I told you about?" Clint asked.

Just then, the confusion cleared away from Dell's face like clouds parting to show the sun. "You told me you fixed that rifle Jeremiah found so that it wouldn't fire."

"No, I told you I fixed it so that it would backfire. Whoever fired that rifle was the killer we were after or he was in league with the killer. Either way, he deserved whatever he got for pulling that trigger."

Clint had explained what would happen to the deputy moments before Niedelander arrived. Even so, seeing the plan in action was enough to rattle the deputy right down to the core. It was also the last piece of evidence that Dell had been after. That backfire happened just as Clint said it would, meaning that Niedelander had been the one to kill the man at Clint's feet outside of that restaurant.

It also meant that Niedelander had been the one to benefit the most from covering up what that same man had been about to say.

The implications went on from there, getting worse and worse every step of the way. Whatever doubt remained was being wiped clean by the rants coming from Niedelander's own mouth.

"Those girls died happy!" Niedelander shouted through the pain grating through the front half of his body. "I saw to it that they died happy! I didn't do anything wrong! Those girls were happy!"

As he said that, Niedelander used the back of his left hand to swipe away the blood trickling into his eyes. With his right hand, he reached for a gun stuck under his belt in a spot that had been hidden by his jacket.

Clint saw the motion and reached for his own modified Colt. He couldn't get to the Colt right away because of the way he'd landed when jumping to one side. After a quick shift, he cleared leather.

Niedelander was just a little quicker.

The draw was quick and efficient, reminding Clint of a practiced, military move. Between the smoke in the air and the blood in his eyes, Niedelander was able to squeeze off a quick shot rather than an accurate one.

Lead hissed through the air past Clint's head, passing by far enough away to keep from doing any harm, but close enough to make him duck while squeezing off a shot of his own. Niedelander was still reeling in pain, but kept his head enough to step out of the house and disappear into the darkness.

"You all right, Dell?" Clint asked.

The deputy was obviously shaken, but he did a good job of holding himself together. "Yeah. I'm not hit. What about you?"

"Nope," Clint said as he crouched low and started moving toward the back of the house. "Not yet, anyway."

Before reaching the door, Clint stopped and pressed his back against a wall. He'd seen enough to know that Niedelander wasn't anything close to what he appeared to be. He was no meek wallflower and he was most certainly not a stranger around a gunfight.

Clint was a bit surprised that his alterations to the rifle had gone unnoticed, but it would have taken an expert's eye to spot the minor flaw he'd created. That flaw was like a well-placed hairline crack in a support beam. One bit of pressure in the wrong direction was all it had taken for that crack to send everything else tumbling down around it.

He smirked to himself as he leaned back against the wall. Reaching out, Clint picked up a Bible that had been laying on a table nearby and tossed it toward the door. Sure enough, as soon as the good book hit the frame, a shot came from outside to punch a hole in the wood.

Clint recognized the sound of the shot as a pistol. Apparently, Niedelander was still in the habit of carrying his holdout gun just in case his main weapon was compromised. Military men may have been deadly fighters, but they were easier to read than a newspaper.

That didn't mean that Niedelander would go down easily, though. On the contrary, Clint figured the ex–cavalry officer knew every inch of terrain around his home like the back of his hand. He'd probably already scouted out every possible escape route and vantage point months ago.

All of that left Clint with precious few options. One of them was doing something Niedelander wouldn't expect. Of course, the only reason such an action wouldn't be expected would be because only a damn fool would do it.

With precious seconds ticking away, Clint threw common sense out the window and went in for the kill.

FORTY-FIVE

Killing Adams wasn't a part of Niedelander's plan, but it wasn't an unwelcome change either. Instead, he thought of it more as a bonus. All of his other kills were sweet and soft as freshly baked pie. This one would be like a well-cooked steak.

Actually, considering the fight Adams was bound to put up, that steak would be rare. Niedelander could already taste the blood in his mouth.

Having discarded the rifle, Niedelander cursed himself for not checking over the gun twice rather than just once. The scars on his face would be a good reminder of that mistake so he would never make it again. His gun hand was already wrapped around the same pistol that he'd carried into battle on several occasions. It hadn't let him down before, so he knew it wouldn't let him down now.

Niedelander waited in the shadow he'd picked, knowing better than to break cover, in case Adams was watching. It would almost be a shame to kill Adams. Going up against someone like that was always such a disappointment. Usually the most dangerous men turned out to be so little in the end.

That was why Niedelander had decided to set his sights

179

on a different prey. A prey that appealed to another sort of instinct rather than his love of killing.

Niedelander loved all the girls his blade had touched.

In the end, when their eyes had glazed over, he'd known that they loved him, too.

A window was opening on the side of the house. It was a quiet, subtle movement, but Niedelander had picked it out. There was a rustling inside the house as Dell moved for the front door. Niedelander could see through the back doorway all the way to the front. By the looks of it, the deputy meant to come around one side of the house while Adams slipped out the window to cover the other side.

It was a classic flanking maneuver. Against almost any other opponent, it probably would have worked.

But not this time.

Niedelander settled back into his shadow and lifted his gun. He had the luxury of picking his target, so he got ready to pick off the most dangerous of the two right away. Surely, there would be a distraction meant to catch his attention and then the real attack would come.

The window slid open a little more.

Something stirred inside the house.

The front door came open and Dell hurried outside. Niedelander figured it would take the deputy about thirty seconds to sneak around to a good position.

The window was propped open now and something flew through the air. Sure enough, it was another book aimed for the back door frame. The distraction had arrived and Niedelander took a shot at it so the other two would think their plan was going along right on schedule.

Once the book hit the ground, Niedelander shifted his aim toward the window and prepared to kill the first thing to climb out of it.

There were some heavy steps and some movement from the edge of Niedelander's vision. Something else was charging through the back door and heading straight for him and it wasn't another book.

Clint kept his head down low and rushed forward like a bull with its tail on fire. His modified Colt was held out in front of him and aimed at the general area where he figured Niedelander was hiding.

He knew he would only get one clean shot before Niedelander moved or fired at him, so Clint held out to make that shot count.

Every instinct in his head was screaming for Clint to fire, but he held off until taking the third step out of the house. Holding the Colt at hip level, Clint fired off a round.

Niedelander stumbled out of the shadow, lifting his pistol in front of him.

By this time, Dell had charged around the other side of the house, firing a shot which dug a messy hole into the dirt. "Surrender your gun, Ernie!" the deputy shouted.

But Niedelander was way past listening to anything other than the demons in his own mind. He fired a quick shot at Clint, intended to buy him another second in which to aim properly.

Unlike most anyone else in that situation, Clint didn't falter and he didn't so much as twitch at the incoming bullet. Instead, he extended his arm as though he was going to point a finger at Niedelander's forehead. That finger, however, was wrapped around the Colt's trigger.

The modified pistol bucked in Clint's hand, spitting out a tongue of smoke while sending a single round through Niedelander's skull.

Blood and brains filled the air in a pulpy mist as Niedelander staggered on his feet. He looked more surprised than anything else, allowing his gun to slip from his hand as he dropped down to his knees.

"I . . . loved them," Niedelander whispered as his eyes rolled up into his head. "All nineteen of them."

Dell rushed up to point his gun at the dead man. When Niedelander finally dropped, Dell let out the breath he'd been holding and lowered his pistol. "Jesus. How could I not have known? He was right here and I never knew. How could I let that happen?"

Clint could barely speak. The disgust and anger he felt at the sight of Niedelander made every muscle in his body tense. At that moment, the only thing he wanted was for Niedelander to get up so he could kill him again.

"Do me a favor, Dell."

"Name it."

"Speak up at Allison's trial and tell the judge that Niedelander admitted to killing her sister and the rest of those girls. If any of this bastard's friends were half as bad as him, she doesn't deserve to hang for killing them."

Dell was hesitant, but he nodded. "Yeah. I think you're right. After what we've seen here, I don't think anyone on God's green earth would blame her for hunting down this piece of trash." He shook his head and let the shakes come over him. "Nineteen. He was talking about nineteen different girls?"

"That's be my guess," Clint responded tensely. From there, he holstered his Colt and walked away.

"Where are you going?" Dell asked.

"To tell Jeremiah what happened here. That man deserves a bit of good news after all the hell he's been through."

Watch for

THE GHOST OF GOLIAD

286th novel in the exciting GUNSMITH series

from Jove

Coming in October!

J. R. ROBERTS

THE GUNSMITH

GIANT ACTION! GIANT ADVENTURE!

THE GUNSMITH

GIANT

GIANT WESTERNS FEATURING THE GUNSMITH

THE GHOST OF BILLY THE KID
0-515-13622-0

LITTLE SURESHOT AND THE WILD WEST SHOW
0-515-13851-7

AVAILABLE WHEREVER BOOKS ARE SOLD OR AT PENGUIN.COM

J799

Explore the exciting Old West with one of the men who made it wild!